THE GUILT

A novel

EDWARD SCHWARTZ

iUniverse, Inc.
New York Bloomington

THE GUILT

This is a work of fiction. All of the characters, names, incidents, organizations, and dialogue in this novel are either the products of the author's imagination or are used fictitiously.
iUniverse books may be ordered through booksellers or by contacting:

iUniverse
1663 Liberty Drive
Bloomington, IN 47403
www.iuniverse.com
1-800-Authors (1-800-288-4677)

ISBN: 9-781-4401-1468-7 (pbk)
ISBN: 9-781-4401-1469-4 (ebk)

Printed in the United States of America

iUniverse rev. date: 12/30/2008

For David

Acknowledgments

I am greatly indebted to rabbi Moshe Miller. His book *ZOHAR* inspired me to spread my wings; without it, my novel *THE GUILT* would never have been started, and would never have been finished.

I would also to thank a gifted artist, Igor Pustovalov, who designed the book cover.

BOOKS BY EDWARD SCHWARTZ

KALEIDOSCOPE
DREAMS COME AT TWILIGHT
COLORS OF ETERNITY
EMBRACING THE WORLD
A DEEP DANGER
DO NOT THINK ABOUT TOMORROW
INSIDE THE RAINBOW
ONE STEP FORWARD, TWO STEPS BACKWARD
THE CASE OF DONALD HUSE
PRETEND YOU ARE HAPPY
THE WHITE CLIFF
RAINBOW BEHIND THE BACK
SEEKING THE FIREBIRD'S NEST
JEWISH BLOOD
DESTRUCTION
THE GUILT

"On that day God will be One, and His name One."

– Zechariah 14: 9

1.

Inspector Jacob Reterseil, called by his fellow police officers Jack, was a keen, shrewd man, gifted with remarkable foresight and general prescience. He was commonly regarded as a comer in the department, but not everyone admired his directness or his strongly fixed ideas about detective work.

The phone rang just as he was about to leave his office. Picking up the receiver, he gave his usual, "Reterseil."

"Hi, Jack! I knew you'd still be at the office, aligning with positive energy." Captain O'Burke's voice echoed with kidding notes.

Jacob kept silent. Today he was too tired to continue their usual half-ironical interchange of words.

"Listen, Jack," O'Burke continued after a pause, seriously. "Do me a favor. A prominent rabbi from Boro Park is dead. Nothing unusual, seventy-seven years old. You have to know better than I do how sensitive these people are in this type of case. I'd like you to sign the final report stating that the cause of death was natural," he said, hinting at Jack's being Jewish.

"I have to know it better than you do, John," Jacob conciliated. "Where's the body?"

"In the Kings County Hospital morgue."

"Why's it so urgent?"

"The burial is scheduled for tomorrow," O'Burke said. He wanted to add, 'it's your rules,' but bit his tongue.

Captain O'Burke had become the NYPD Special Homicide Division commanding officer only seven months before. He couldn't say he liked Jacob very much although the man was one of his best detectives. He couldn't say also he didn't respect Jacob whose colleagues called him "wizard" for his extraordinary analytical ability. It wasn't personal. Captain O'Burke was brought up and raised in a poor Catholic neighborhood, in atmosphere of anti-Semitic prejudices.

"Okay, John," Jacob said, reading the silence.

As he hung up, he thought about recent changes in the department. From time to time, some transformations had taken place in police headquarters composition. But they were not significant. There were wheels within wheels, the existence of some of which he could only guess, but they had seldom produced unexpected results. O'Burke's call was caused not so much by the urgent need to sign the paper, but by his willingness to receive his boss' credit for good relations with the Jewish community. Jacob knew that before O'Burke was transferred to headquarters, he had a successful career due to his ability to complete his tasks in a professional manner. In the headquarters, he had to study the art of massaging the ego of his boss, Deputy Police Commissioner Ryan Huskey. Captain O'Burke was not too happy about it.

Jacob put the files from his desk into the safe and left the office. The Homicide Division – a big, open room with a dozen battered desks pushed up close to one another – was almost empty this time of the evening, not counting three officers finishing their paper work.

"Buy, guys," Jacob said, going out.

It was a nice summer evening. The wind hurried isolated clouds across the sky. Yesterday's moisture had gone, and the air had an unusually natural taste for the center of Manhattan. Jacob took several deep breaths and headed for the garage.

From downtown Police Plaza, it took him only twenty minutes to reach the Kings County Hospital as the traffic through the Brooklyn Bridge was not too heavy this time of the evening. But it was already dark when Jacob parked his car. He went to the entrance and showed his ID badge to the hospital guard.

"Where is the morgue?"

The guard, a shapeless, oversized female told him the way, but her English was so poor that Jacob could only guess what she had told.

"How could she be hired to a hospital police if she can hardly move?" Jacob thought as he entered to the freight elevator that would take him to the basement.

To find the morgue was difficult. Several times Jacob lost his way in the labyrinth of the hospital's basement, empty this late time. At last he saw the sign, 'Mortuary.'

*

A sleepy attendant looked at the intruder with one arched brow, but he nodded when Jacob showed his ID.

"Yaakov Lieberman," Jacob said.

The attendant opened his log. He looked over the list of

names. Then he approached a wall of small doors and pulled out a gurney.

"All yours," he said as he waved casually at the shrouded figure.

Jacob came closer and folded the linen from the face of the dead man. The face was calm and still held the nobility of a clever man. Automatically Jacob said a short prayer.

"The death is due to natural causes," Jacob remembered O'Burke's words. "Nothing unusual, the rabbi was seventy-seven."

Jacob looked through the medical examiner's report briefly. My father's the same age, Jacob thought. He was about to put the drape back. But instead, he pulled the cloth down to the waist. He couldn't explain why he did it. It was a sudden impulse.

Jacob shuddered. On the dead man's chest, he saw a livid spot in the shape of the Hebrew letter *alef*. It wasn't a fresh mark. It would be fairer to call it pale. But it was visible without glasses. How could the medical examiner ignore this? Jack put his glasses on. There was no doubt – the spot had the shape of the letter *alef*.

"Nonsense," Jacob muttered, I'm too tired." He covered the body and left the morgue.

Why had the medical examiner omitted this livid spot from his report? The thought repeated itself as Jacob made his way to the car. I am definitely too tired. It was illusion, he told himself.

He sat in the car for a few minutes, submerged in his thoughts. But then, instead of driving away, Jacob returned to the morgue. The attendant looked up at Jacob with surprise.

"Do you need another body?"

"The same one. Switch all the lights on, please."

Jacob jerked the linen off the body. There were no visible marks or livid spots on it. The medical examiner's report was correct. But Jacob could have sworn on the Torah that several minutes ago he had seen that livid spot in the shape of the letter *alef*. He carefully covered the dead rabbi's body. Reluctantly, he turned away and walked back to his car.

*

Sitting in the car, Jacob thought a drink would be definitely useful for him. Not a glass of the kosher Manischewitz wine that he could get in Boro Park, but something stronger. Starting the car, Jacob drove along the street until he stopped the car near the first bar he could find – The Irish Pub.

Jacob went in, sat at the bar counter, and ordered vodka on the rocks. Waiting for a drink, he pondered over what his own life had been: New York, police investigations, his recent painful divorce from Gwendolyn… Looking around, he noted that the bar was full. A big Irish Day parade would take place the next day, he remembered. But the Irish people have already begun their celebration. His drink arrived, and Jacob took a gulp.

I'm tired, I need a rest, he thought. Three new murder cases on my desk and investigations I haven't finished yet are more than enough for me. In one case, I have no clue about what was the motif of a crime. That's the rare case in my practice. Jacob took another gulp, but didn't feel any heat in his stomach. Maybe I'm getting old – I'm already forty-one. He sighed. Luckily, we had no children, he muttered, remembering Gwendolyn's face.

Jacob took another gulp and, at last, felt a pleasant heat

in his stomach. He was tired, but not exhausted. His fellow-policemen consider him a strong man. He has to be strong. Jacob finished the first glass, caught the eye of the bartender, and ordered another.

Suddenly his recollections again highlighted the letter *alef* on the chest of the dead rabbi. He mentally reviewed what he had seen.

"It was illusion," he said aloud as he tried to persuade himself.

Jacob's words woke the man who was napping nearby. The fellow raised his head and looked at Jacob with muddy, drunken eyes.

"A Jew?" he asked indifferently, seeing a *kipa* on Jacob's head.

"A Jew," Jacob agreed, also indifferently.

"Get out of here, Jew," the man said casually.

"Fuck you," Jacob said good-naturedly.

With a frown, the man tried to hit at Jacob with his left hand. It was a moment for the fast action. The man was bigger and potentially stronger than Jacob, but Jacob was quicker. Smashing his glass on the edge of the bar, he pushed it into the man's face.

Three Irish men jumped up to teach a lesson to the impudent fellow, but Jacob pulled a gun from its holster and flashed his police ID.

"Go back, slums!"

Jacob ordered another drink and threw it down his throat. Then he paid for drinks and went toward the door.

Returning home, Jacob called Captain O'Burke.

"John, I've been in Kings County."

"And put your signature on the paper?"

"No."

"Why?"

"I am not a hundred percent sure the death was natural." Jacob rubbed his forehead, feeling a headache coming on.

"Are you crazy?"

"A little bit."

"What's the percentage of your doubt, Jack?"

"One percent."

"Are you kidding me? It's not very funny."

"It was not intended as a joke, John. But it would be better if you ask Larry Brown to sign that paper. Good night," Jacob said and hung up.

2.

Jacob Reterseil couldn't explain why he drove to Boro Park to attend the Rabbi Yaakov Lieberman's burial the next afternoon. Until the lunch hour, he had been busy at the office. He had to attend a routine meeting conducted by Deputy Police Commissioner Ryan Huskey, a tall, arrogant man of sixty years old, who dreamed of being a commissioner one day.

He was responsible for improving the image of the police force in the eyes of the Orthodox Jewish community. After an Australian Orthodox Jew Yankel Rosenbaum was killed in Boro Park by a mob of black youngsters, a seemingly permanent tension between blacks and whites existed on the Boro Park streets.

"The only order of business for today's meeting is how to keep the peace on Boro Park streets during Rabbi Lieberman's funeral," Ryan Huskey declared.

The meeting was routine and formal. There was no sense in reminding police officers of their duties, but Ryan Huskey wanted to secure his back in case of street disorder.

"What do we want?" he asked the attendees. "We want

the people of Boro Park to look after the youngsters of Boro Park."

Ryan Huskey didn't say 'black youngsters,' but all the attendees knew what political correctness meant. He was playing the same old game...

Jacob listened to Ryan Huskey absent-mindedly. None of the attendees asked questions, considering the meeting a waste of time.

"We must do our job with clear conscience," Ryan Huskey finalized his speech.

Jacob grinned. Every guilty man talks about clear conscience, he thought, recalling that Ryan Huskey had been the commanding officer in the Boro Park precinct when Yankel Rosenbaum was killed.

*

Knowing that the burial had to start early, Jacob hadn't considered taking part in it; rather he wanted to talk to someone who knew the late Rabbi Yaakov Lieberman.

It turned out that the ceremony had been postponed, waiting for Rabbi Yaakov Lieberman's son Eli who lived in Millburn, Australia, where he was a rabbi in an Orthodox synagogue. The flight from Millburn to New York lasted more than twenty hours, but an unexpected gusty wind forced the plane to be rerouted to Boston. From there Rabbi Eli Lieberman had to take a train to get to New York.

In spite of the fact that Jacob wore a *kipa*, he looked like a foreigner among the thousands of people who filled the streets close to the synagogue. He looked more like a Reform than an Orthodox Jew, and sometimes caught surprising glances, "What's this guy doing here?"

The late Rabbi Yaakov Lieberman was a highly respected man. Many Boro Park residents considered him a *tzaddik* or a holy man. His modest house was always open to anyone who needed his advice or even money. He was also respected as a rabbinical schoolteacher who shared his deep knowledge of the Torah with his students. Even the late Lubavicher leader Rebbe Menachem Schneerson often asked him for a piece of advice in his interpretations of the Oral Torah. For these reasons, thousands of people gathered in the Boro Park streets to pay their last respects to the late rabbi.

Looking at all the people in the street, Jacob thought this man could not have had any enemies wishing him dead. I have to discard my doubts – the rabbi died with a natural death, Jacob thought. My work has made me crazy. I look like an idiot who doesn't trust his own father.

As he thought of his father, Jacob knew that his attendance at Rabbi Lieberman's burial was only a reason to visit his father.

Jacob's father, Doctor and Rabbi Moses Reterseil, was a descendant of a highly respected Hungarian family that had given Hungary many well-known rabbis and thinkers. Most of the family had perished in the fire of the Holocaust. Moses Reterseil was lucky: his father had managed to leave Hungary and immigrate to the U.S. at the beginning of the century. Was everything forecast from Above?

Moses graduated from Yeshiva University Medical School. Later he finished a Rabbinical School, but dedicated most of his life to treating Jews in Boro Park. Blessed with a daughter and a son, he could be considered a happy man.

Moses' daughter had married a cantor of one of the numerous Boro Park synagogues, and he became a happy grandfather of three girls. But he couldn't be considered a happy father of his son Jacob.

Jacob grew into a clever and independently thinking boy. In spite of being at the top of his class in his yeshiva and having a crystal clear future, Jacob unexpectedly declared that he was not going to attend a rabbinical school.

"Are you going to attend a medical school then?" asked Moses, thinking that his son would follow in his footsteps.

"No, dad. I'm going to NYU Law School," Jacob said, glaring at his father openly.

"Are you attracted to collecting money, son?" Moses asked, surprised. "In that case, it's a strange decision. There's almost no crime in our community."

"The world is not restricted to the boundaries of our community, dad; it's wider," Jacob objected. "It is possible to spend your whole life inside the synagogue, leaning over books, but not becoming a Jew."

"Those are strange thoughts for a young Jewish man," Moses said thoughtfully. "There is no Law but the Law of Torah, and the laws of any civilized society are based on the Torah." As Jacob kept silent, Moses added, "Now you are a rebellious teenager. I would be happy if you changed your mind."

Jacob didn't change his mind. He had entered the school of his choice. Giving tribute to the laws of society beyond Boro Park, he took off the traditional Hassidim suit in favor of a traditional European one. The only attribute to his Jewishness, a *kipa,* remained on his head. He was not going to become a self-hating Jew; he was proud of what he had been.

Moses turned out to be right in his worst predicaments: living in a society, nobody can be free of it.

"Jacob has stopped being a Jew," he said bitterly to his wife Leah when Jacob moved to the NYU dormitory.

Moses knew what he was talking about. When Jacob married, against his father's wish, Gwendolyn, a charming blonde of Swedish decent, he had finally stopped being an Orthodox Jew.

They created a strange married couple. At the High Holidays, Jacob went to synagogue, while his wife Gwendolyn went to church. God didn't bless Jacob's marriage, as he and Gwendolyn had no children. Having no spiritual intimacy, what did they have that was mutual except for sexual intimacy?

Gwendolyn was emotionally reserved, a dry young lady, but she was the first and the only woman in Jacob's life. Was it love or only amorousness of a pure soul? This question didn't come to his mind for a long time, and Jacob had no chance to compare her with anyone else. He persuaded himself that he loved Gwendolyn.

Why did he marry her without his father's blessing? Jacob knew it would be a shock to his parents. He had done it because he knew Moses would never give his blessing. Marrying a *shiksa* had meant for Moses that his son no longer being a Jew.

Jacob was wrong. His father was more democratic in his views than most of men of his generation. Although Moses considered such a marriage was not the best case scenario for his son, it would be acceptable for him in case if Gwendolyn would pass *giur*.

Jacob didn't ask Gwendolyn about it; he knew that she wouldn't agree to become a Jewish woman – she was too much a Christian. So they both kept a *status quo* for many years until, naturally, their marriage had broken.

After graduating from the NYU law school, Jacob applied to the police academy without telling anyone. The only cadet wearing a *kipa*, he graduated at the top of his class. It was not only because of his wit that he had won the other cadets' respect, but also by his achievements in martial arts.

Again unexpectedly, even for his wife Gwendolyn, Jacob submitted an application for a position in the police department homicide division. He was hired. Not because of his impressive resume; mainly because the personal department bureaucrats were afraid of a lawsuit based on religious discrimination if he were rejected.

By the time of Captain O'Burke's call, Jacob was one of the leading police headquarters detectives, and the nickname "wizard" had become his business card.

My father is definitely among these mourners, Jacob thought, looking at the sea of people around him. When this is over, I would have to visit him.

*

As a burial procedure was postponed, Jacob returned to the police headquarters. On the way to his office, in the hall leading to the interrogation rooms, he met Captain O'Burke.

"Hi, Jack! Have you kept your doubts about the cause of the rabbi's death?" O'Burke's lips turned up in a grin.

"I have, John," Jacob replied honestly.

"Can you tell me why?" O'Burke asked, trying to keep his voice neutral, avoiding an unpleasant demeanor.

"I am afraid not, captain. I can't explain it even to myself. It's just a feeling, my intuition," Jacob said. He was glad to be able to be truthful.

"Intuition cannot be filed, Jack," O'Burke commented. "Without facts, there's not even a hypothesis. Forget about it. An old man has died. Such things happen." Then he added ironically, "It was God's will, wasn't it?"

Not waiting for Jacob's response, O'Burke turned toward the hall, heading to his office.

"God's will," Jacob repeated thoughtfully as he remembered the letter *alef* on the dead rabbi's chest.

Then he went to his office. Back at his desk, he sorted through the paperwork that had accumulated on it. A scattering of half-formed thoughts flitted through Jacob's head. Discarding them, he took one of the files from the safe and placed it carefully in the center of his desk. Then he opened it to look at a photo of a man on the front sheet. It wasn't a face of a criminal, just an ordinary face of an ordinary man. Not clever, not stupid, no different from other faces. Why did this idiot kill his father? The man confessed that he hated his father, but sworn to God that he had not committed the crime. If he hadn't, who framed him and why? Looking at the photo, Jacob was preoccupied until he came to the conclusion he was cozying up to the wrong idea of the man's guilt.

Who knew that the man hated his father? It was too personal to confess to anyone that he hated the man who had given him life. How could a man hate his father? He had to be inhuman… Jacob's half-formed thoughts returned to his father. Now they were perfectly formed. He, Jacob, prayed to Lord every day and asked for forgiveness for the pain that he had caused his father.

Why did he, Jacob, cause his father's suffering? He justified it by his self-confirmation. What a stupid word! To prove in his own eyes that he could be tougher than everyone around him? He did it. They consider him a member of the police family. He has bided his time in the service of justice. But was that his goal? What had he spent the last fifteen years of his life on? Jacob rubbed his forehead as if trying to relieve a headache. He helped to send hundreds of criminals to jail, and a dozen of them to an electric chair. Had society become better because of his work? What was the sense of washing the deck while the ship was sinking? Jacob was full of sad thoughts.

Jacob's thoughts might have continued this backward spiral if something hadn't suddenly highlighted his mind. He again looked at the face of the man suspected of his father's murder.

"No, he didn't do it. The man had told the truth." Jacob came to an impulsive conclusion.

Jacob stroked his head. This man's son was the only one who could have known about his father's hatred. He was the only one who could have received a profit from his grandfather's death – the family's money.

But he's only sixteen years old! Jacob tried to convince himself that a boy couldn't be so evil at that young age. But he already knew that his intuition was right – the boy had killed his grandfather and framed his father.

Jacob's mood plummeted. He closed the folder, put it back into the safe, and made his way out of the office. He needed a drink. One drink – not a big deal; his father would not notice the smell.

3.

It was not easy to park a car on the street in spite of the fact that the letters NYPD were on Jacob's license plate. The street was too narrow. Cars were parked bumper to bumper, and Jacob found the only empty spot near a fire hydrant. He parked the car and got out.

Walking around the corner, he came to a small, modest house. Its paint was peeling and shingles were missing from the roof. A warm feeling flooded him; he had lived here for almost half his life. His mind engrossed with memories. Life in your parents' house is the happiest part of human life, he thought as he rang the doorbell.

The door opened to reveal Bertha, Jacob's distant relative, standing on the threshold. She was his father's third cousin. The only member of the Reterseil family who had survived the Holocaust, she had lived with Jacob's parents for many years, helping Moses' wife Leah to take care of the family.

Naturally, after Leah's death from an unexpected heart attack fifteen years ago, Bertha continued to take care of the house and of Moses, who remained a big child, far from the reality of life. Although Moses had grown accustomed to Bertha as a part of the house itself, he loved this silent, wrinkled, old woman who had become a part of his family. If anybody told Moses that he should be grateful to Bertha for dedication of her life to him, he would be sincerely surprised: Bertha was a part of him. Why would you be grateful to your limb or heart?

"Jacob!" Bertha embraced him and kissed his cheek. "A rare guest is the most pleasant one," she said. She was a clever woman. "Moses, Jacob has come!" she yelled as Moses' hearing had begun to deteriorate with his years. "You are just on time, my boy," she added. "We're going to have dinner."

When Jacob came into the dining room, Moses was already sitting at table. Every time Jacob saw his father, he seemed to be smaller and more shriveled.

"Seventy-seven," he remembered O'Burke's words. "Things happen." Jack felt a lump in his throat.

"Hi, dad!" He came to Moses and kissed him on the cheek. "I'm happy to see you in such great shape."

"So am I, son. Thanks for coming," Moses said. Tears sparkled in his eyes.

A warm family atmosphere enveloped the diners. Jacob felt the long-forgotten sensation. When he praised Bertha's cooking, she smiled.

"You are already a stranger to healthy Jewish food, my boy," she said. "Your *shiksa* could take better care of you, taking into account that the way to a man's heart is through his stomach."

"He is divorced, Bertha," Moses reminded her casually.

"Sorry, I forgot. I am becoming absent-minded," she agreed.

"The charm of the past is in the past." Jacob smiled. He was in good spirits.

After dinner Moses and Jacob went to the study. Jacob sat in his favorite old chair and looked around. All the walls were covered with bookshelves. Nothing had changed in the house since his happy childhood. Nothing had changed in the room except for the big picture of his late mother on the wall. Jacob gazed at the picture. How beautiful his mother was! Only now he saw that his mother had the facial features of a Jewish goddess, was as beautiful as Leah or Sarah could be.

"I attended Rabbi Lieberman's funeral today," Jacob said to interrupt the silence.

Moses looked at him with surprise. "Did you know him?"

"No."

"Then what was the reason for your attendance? Curiosity?"

"Professional curiosity, dad."

"What can be curious about an old man's death?" Moses asked, looking at his son attentively.

"Nothing," Jacob agreed. "My boss Captain O'Burke asked me to sign a paper stating that Rabbi Lieberman's death was from natural causes," he explained.

As he paused, Moses asked, "And?"

"I did not."

"Why?"

"I can't explain it. Something had stopped me." Jacob sighed.

"What do you call *something*, Jacob?" Moses asked, immediately intrigued.

For a moment Jacob was startled by the definiteness of the question. He found no immediate words to reply. Then he told Moses about the letter *alef* that he had seen on Rabbi Lieberman's chest.

"I'm not even sure that I really saw it. Maybe it was illusion. When I went back to the morgue, I saw nothing. Nothing at all!" Jacob exclaimed emotionally. He took a long pause, being submerged in recollections of the previous night. "I'm trying to persuade myself that it wasn't real, but it was, dad. I can swear on the Torah that I've seen it. It wasn't illusion, but if I tell anybody in my office about it, they would laugh at me," he said with increasing volume.

Moses listened carefully to the story that Jacob told him. The more he heard the more excited he became. He stood up and paced from one end of the room to the other, murmuring something as he became submerged in his own thoughts and did not hear Jacob. But he hadn't missed a word of Jacob's story. Moses took a deep breath, his excitement mounting. His face danced with anticipation for the briefest of instants. At last Moses stopped, took his glasses off, and looked at Jacob.

"It wasn't illusion, son," he said firmly.

"What?" Jacob asked with a bit of surprise.

"I am more than assured in it." Moses nodded and sucked in another breath; he looked very excited.

"What do you mean, dad?" Jacob leaned forward and gazed at the faraway look in his father's eyes. His father obviously wanted to say more.

"I think someone made an attempt at soul transfusion," Moses said almost casually. He had already suppressed his emotions.

"Soul transfusion? Dad, we live in the twenty-first century!" Jacob shrugged, challenging him with a difficult smile.

"That's right, son. But we know no more about God's creation than we knew in the eleventh century; maybe even less." Moses' eyes regarded Jacob thoughtfully.

"What do you call 'soul transfusion'?" Jacob asked.

"I'll try to explain it in habitual meaning for you, son. What we call 'understandable,' in reality is only what is acceptable to understand, like blood transfusion, for instance. Blood is a part of body; the soul is as well; the only difference – blood is a physical part, soul is spiritual. Both are unique and given by God. If He allowed the transfusion of one of the physical forms, why not suggest that, *under the special conditions*, He would allow making the transfusion of the spiritual form?" Moses asked, accenting words *under the special conditions*. He sounded very serious.

"It's beyond my understanding, dad. That's already for mystics," Jacob said thoughtfully.

"I can't agree with you, Jacob. People call 'mystics' everything that is beyond their understanding. But it's only a lack of knowledge. It would be more correct to say that 'mystics' is a meaning for people who haven't yet reached the proper level of education," Moses said.

As Jacob kept silent, Moses continued, "One simple example is *Zohar*. The history of publishing that book is the most intrigued enigma of Jewish history. The book was distributed for the first time at the end of the thirteenth century by the Spanish cabalist Moshe de Leon. He stated that the book he had put on sale was a copy of an ancient manuscript written by Rashbi in the second century. In 1305, in the city of Valladolid, he had met a young cabalist from Israel, Itzhak Ben-Schmuel. He invited Ben-Shmuel to visit his home and promised to show him the ancient original of Rashbi's manuscript. But on the way home, Moshe de Leon met an unexpected death. This, however, didn't stop young Ben-Schmuel, who was eager to see the ancient manuscript. He reached de Leon's home and asked his widow to show him the priceless manuscript." Moses paused and smiled as he saw the skeptical move of Jacob's lips. Then he continued. "I see that you want to ask me a question, Jacob, how do we know this? We know it from the diary that Ben-Schmuel left, where he had described his search." Moses took a big gulp of water from the glass on his desk as if the story made his mouth dry.

Jacob didn't interrupt his father's narrative. He hasn't yet understood how this story would be associated to the death of Rabbi Lieberman.

Mosses glanced at Jacob's face and continued the story, "But de Leon's widow extended her hands in surprise. 'There is no ancient manuscript,' she told Ben-Schmuel. 'My husband wrote the book himself. He made Rashbi the book's author for commercial purposes as he wanted the book to be in great demand on the market.'

Naturally the question is who told the truth and who lied?" Moses asked cunningly. "What do you think?"

"What do I think?" Jacob repeated thoughtfully. "On one side, Moshe de Leon could hardly have known the day of his death. In that case, what was the sense of his lying if he couldn't show Ben-Schmuel the manuscript? From the other side, de Leon's wife wouldn't know where her husband had hid the manuscript. She could also be afraid that the manuscript could be stolen or could dream that her late husband would be honored as the author."

"You are giving voice to my thoughts, Jacob." Moses laughed. "Now I realized that you work for the police department. Your logic is irreproachable." Then he continued his story. "The woman didn't persuade Ben-Schmuel. He continued searching for the original, describing his search in the diary until... his diary stopped in the most interesting place; it kept all the questions open."

"And who was recognized as the author of *Zohar*?" Jacob's curiosity was sincere.

"The academic point of view and that of traditional Judaism are different. The book language sometimes does not correspond to that of the second century; neither does its Aramaic language. Moshe de Leon could have made some changes working on the book, but..." Moses stopped and sighed.

Jacob didn't interrupt the silence, being submerged in the mysterious story. After a deep, uninterrupted silence, Moses continued his story again.

"But I am an adherent of another version. Our cabalistic books describe a method of joining the soul of a dead *tzaddik*. I am more than assured that Moshe de Leon, who studied the *Kabbalah* very seriously and wrote several books on the subject, should use this method to join Rashbi's soul. He wrote '*Sefer ha Zohar*' as he reached the state of a 'medium.' In that condition, he only wrote what Rashbi had dictated to him." A fierce light burned in Moses' eyes as he told the story.

A thousand thoughts rioted through the brain of the eager, attentive Jacob, but he uttered no word; he wouldn't interrupt his father. Moses caught the quick, impatient movement of his face.

"I think it's hardly possible, dad, even in the state of a 'medium,'" Jacob said at last, thoughtfully. I can recognize that de Leon could talk to Rashbi for a short time, but to write a book... impossible."

"It's impossible for all cases but one, son. If de Leon was not *contacted* to Rashbi's soul, but was *connected* to her. A contact is a short-time action while a connection is long. To reach a contact, you can use drugs, such as opium or even some kind of mushrooms. For instance, remember Carlos Castaneda's experience."

"Carlos Castaneda?"

"His name was on the lips of a whole generation only forty years ago. In his books, he had offered people the way to reach a new reality. Not surprising that you don't know his name, Jacob." Moses grinned. Then he continued, "But to reach the connection of souls…Maybe only de Leon managed to experience it and penetrated through the mystery of Torah. Everything depends on the depth of our knowledge, Jacob. *Zohar* is the bottomless source of that knowledge. Try to read this book, Jacob." Moses' eyes became fixed upon space. His mind was searching for something he had recently heard from his son – the letter *alef* on the chest of the dead Rabbi Lieberman. For a brief while he was absorbed in his vision.

"Dad," Jacob returned his father to the reality. "The man who made an attempt at soul transfusion, using your terminology, intentionally or unintentionally killed Rabbi Lieberman. No man can take other man's life and avoid punishment," Jacob said carefully.

"I don't think it was intentionally, Jacob. But who can blame this man? You live in the material world, son. Can you prove it is a murder case? I don't think so. Nobody can." Moses stopped and glanced at Jacob, who shrugged without speaking. So Moses continued, "To even talk to this man, if you find him, you have, at least, to study the *Kabbalah* and read *Zohar*. The Torah says the *Kabbalah* is opened for a beginner who is a man of forty with kids. You are not a proper person, son, to judge this man. Nobody can judge him but God, blessed be His name," Moses said. His face grew moody.

"Success is often the result of taking a misstep in the right direction." Jacob smiled as he tried to avoid the conversation so difficult for him.

But Moses didn't support Jacob's irony.

"What we see depends mainly on what we look for, Jacob. There is a presumption of innocence; you know that better than I do. I know this man is innocent. But I'd like you to find him. Not to punish him. He is a unique man of our generation, who has reached a deeper level of the mystery of God's creation. I'd like to talk to him before I die." Moses eyes were full of an unwanted depression.

Jacob sighed. A myriad of thoughts crowded his brain as he said, "Please be my mentor, dad. Together we'll find the man. It won't be easy. We have to check out all the people who had met Rabbi Lieberman for at least the past year. Did you know Rabbi Lieberman?"

"Everybody did."

"You personally."

"Not too close."

"Maybe his secretary can be useful for us?"

Moses smiled. "His secretary Abe Berger was one of my students at Einstein Medical School."

"Can you ask him to show me his appointment books?"

"I can talk to him if it can help," Moses said thoughtfully.

"It would be wonderful if he gives you his appointment schedules, dad. Then I'll do my part of work and analyze the information."

"Rabbi Lieberman had met hundred and hundred of

people," Moses said doubtfully. "He was a world-famous authority on the *Kabbalah*."

"But we don't have another clue as to how to approach the man," Jacob said firmly. "This is the only way."

"Okay." A smile touched the corners of Moses' lips. "Don't postpone until tomorrow what you can do today," he said. "I'll give him a call now." He picked up a receiver and dialed a number.

"Hi, Abe. This is Dr. Moses Reterseil speaking. I want to ask you about a favor. Among the Rabbi Lieberman's visitors in the past year, there was the author of a book that I've recently read. I'd like to talk to him about the book. Can you check the appointment book for me?"

Abe Berger explained to Moses it wouldn't be possible because several thousand people visited the rabbi in that time frame. And besides, he hadn't the appointment book.

"You don't have it?" Moses surprised.

Abe Berger answered simply that all information was in the computer file.

"Then can you give me a copy of the file, Abe? I'll try to find the man myself. Nothing is difficult for those who have the will to do it." Moses remarked as he tried to make the conversation less formal.

After Abe Berger promised to send Moses a copy of file, he hung up.

"It looks like I've already done part of my work, son," Moses said. He couldn't hide his satisfaction.

"Good job," Jacob agreed with a pleased smile. "Dad, have you ever thought about joining the police department for a part time job?"

"That's a bad idea." Moses retorted.

"Why?"

Moses waited a few seconds before answering.

"It would be a nightmare to have you as my boss, Jacob," Moses said without a smile.

"I'm still not so bad a son," Jacob murmured to himself.

"Anyway, I've done only a part of my task. But if you want me to be your mentor, follow my advice – start reading." Moses came to one of the bookshelves and took out the book. "It's *Zohar*. But it takes a long time to read. Start with this small treatise. I have just finished working on it." He handed Jacob another book.

Jacob opened the thin tome and read the title *The Cabbalistic Treatise about Advantage and Disadvantage of Meal*. He flashed a quick glance of surprise at his father.

Moses smiled mildly.

"Passover is approaching. At any rate, it won't be the worst reading for you, son," he said simply.

Jacob looked at his watch. "I have to go, dad, otherwise Charley's bladder will blown up. My dog walker is off today."

He kissed Moses' cheek and went to the door. Already on the threshold, Jacob asked, "How do you feel, dad?"

"I'm still alive, son." Moses made no move after he'd stopped talking.

The answer was short. Moses didn't want Jacob to hear his trembling voice.

4.

As Jacob was driving home, a mixture of tenderness for his old father and repentance for the pain that he, as his son, had caused him filled his soul. If he was given a chance to start his life over from the beginning, would he choose another way? Was it wrong to seek the own way? His own way... Did it exist? Wasn't the Jewish way of life the one? Wasn't it once and forever defined by God?

Every new generation considered itself cleverer than the previous one; only when we advanced in years, did we realize how stupid we were. Life is too short to make many mistakes. A man who didn't make mistakes did not live, Jacob thought. Maybe vice versa, a man who didn't live did not make mistakes. Jacob grinned to his thoughts. Being obsessed with his self-confirmation, he had missed happiness, a simple man's happiness: love, family, children... This was the only happiness that God had given people. All the rest was and is only the fuss of the fuss. All the rest does not exist. And a man exists only in his children. They were and is the salt of the Earth, Jacob thought bitterly.

Submerged in his thoughts, Jacob drove his car without

haste. A small, sporty, two-door Mercedes SL 600 cut in his lane, and Jacob thought that only a young, rich idiot could drive so aggressively.

The Mercedes was three cars ahead of him when Jacob heard the sound of an impact. The idiot couldn't avoid a collision.

Getting out of his car, Jacob saw the Mercedes door fly open and a woman dash out, running from the scene of the accident. The police officer awoke in Jacob as he ran after the woman, who tried to jump down into the nearest subway entrance. As Jacob grabbed her hand, he caught the sharp odor of alcohol.

"Why are you running, miss?"

A sputter of indignation built up in the woman's throat. Then, seeing a *kipa* on Jacob's head, she hissed spitefully, trying to release his hand, "Don't touch me, fuckin' Jew. Leave me alone."

The prettiest part of her face was the Chanel sunglasses that she wore despite the late time of the day. Why do black people like wearing black glasses at night? Jack wondered automatically as he remembered a Chinese proverb 'You cannot catch a black cat in the dark room.'

"You have to return to your car, miss, and wait for a patrol officer," Jacob said, not feeling any anger.

But despite the fact that the woman could hardly stand on her feet, she tried to smash Jacob's face; he was forced to put handcuffs on her. Jacob removed sunglasses from the woman's face. A slow smile spread across her face, matching the venomous look in her eyes.

"Keep away from me. You will be sorry, fuckin' Jew," the woman hissed again. Her lips parted to release the stench of whisky.

Now Jacob lost his patience. "Watch your mouth, miss. I am a police officer," he said, showing the woman his ID badge.

Still waiting for a cruiser, Jacob briefly searched the Mercedes. As he opened the glove compartment, he found a small package of white powder. He turned it over to the officer when the cruiser arrived.

"She's all yours, sergeant. The whole bucket: alcohol, drugs," Jacob said without looking at the woman.

While they were talking, the second officer had checked the car plate number as the woman did not have a driver license with her. Then he joined Jacob and the sergeant.

"This is 'Princess of Harlem,'" the officer said with a wry smile.

"Who?" Jacob didn't understand him.

"A rap singer," the officer explained. "They like such music. She has already had two accidents under the influence. I think now she's in big trouble." He didn't say 'black people' as he was politically correct.

"Idiotism has no limits," Jacob said with a noticeable droop to his shoulders.

He went to his car. The more we struggle for their rights, the more they hate us, he thought bitterly.

*

When Jacob opened his apartment door, he didn't hear Charley's usual bark, greeting him. As Jacob switched on the light, he saw the dog lay on the floor near the door. He whimpered quietly and looked at Jacob with guilty eyes. Jacob saw a small puddle near him.

"Poor Charley," he said loudly. "It was undeserved

punishment to leave you inside the apartment for the whole day; it's my fault."

The dog looked at him with what appeared to be tears in his eyes. Why are dog's eyes always sad? Jacob wondered.

Then he took a rag and cleaned the floor.

5.

When Jacob came to the office the following day, he caught an early call. He picked up the receiver and heard the voice of Harold Sherman, a celebrity lawyer famous in near-Hollywood circles. Jacob was briefly acquainted with him.

"Hi, Jack!" Harold's voice was as cheerful as the voice of a kid who has recently received a new toy. "This is Harold Sherman, old chap. I think you'll soon see your photo on *The New York Times* pages." As Jacob kept silent, he explained, "You have arrested 'Princess of Harlem.'"

"So what?"

"Listen, Jack, she's a nice kid; a little bit spoiled thanks to her fame, but nice." Harold's voice snapped a bit.

"So what?" Jacob repeated indifferently.

Harold paused. When he continued to talk, cheerful notes of his voice had vanished.

"In your report, you mentioned she had used a racial slur." Harold lowered his voice.

Jacob smiled in the receiver. "Do you like words 'fuckin Jew,' Harold?" he asked ironically.

Harold missed his irony. "Listen, Jack. For driving under

the influence, even on a suspended license, she would be, in the worst case scenario, sentenced to community service and sent to rehab. But if the media makes a point of your report, it can ruin her career."

"Do you want me to apologize to your 'princess,' Harold?"

"Jack, be serious. There is big force behind her. If you want, she'll apologize to you. And you'll rewrite your report without mentioning racial slurs, okay? By the way, her boyfriend is a Jew," Harold added.

"So what?" Jacob asked again. "New York is full of self-hating Jews."

Harold dismissed Jacob's words as if they didn't concern him.

"Is it a deal?" he asked in a worried tone, still half-hopefully.

"Your 'princess' is at an age when she must take responsibility for her actions," Jacob said matter-of-factly. "Unfortunately so-called celebrities are beyond the law. Liberalism had deprived them. Our Jewish liberalism," he added. He felt a little anger rising in him against his will.

"At any case she'll bring you her apology, Jack. She is very sorry," Harold summed up. "You know the 'f' word has so spread in our language that nobody pays attention to it. Please, don't pay attention, Jack. Make the girl happy."

Happiness, Jacob thought as he hung up, what a strange word! Happiness for that 'princess' is narcotics and sex; happiness for his boss, Captain O'Burke, is to become a deputy commissioner; happiness for his father is to discuss eternal questions of God's creation with a mysterious rabbi. Happiness is only man's invention, nothing more. Can a single man be happy?

Jacob finally decided that his first priority would be to find the mysterious man who could be blamed in Rabbi Lieberman's death. But for this job, to concentrate only on this task, he needed time.

Jacob completed an annual leave request and went to Captain O'Burke's office.

"Hi, Jack," O'Burke said, seen Jacob. "Problems?"

"I am not a problem-maker, captain. I am a problem-solver as you say. I'm dead tired, and need a vacation. As I know, crime statistics is down." He sat in the chair and handed O'Burke an annual leave request.

"You are killing me, Jack." O'Burke rubbed at his forehead, trying to relieve a headache as he read the request.

"It's not me; it's Charles Darwin who kills you," Jacob joked. "If according to his stupid theory, work had turned a monkey into a man, it's equally fair to suggest that work also turns a man into a monkey."

But O'Burke didn't appreciate Jacob's humor.

"I am not an adherent of stupid theories, Jack," he said without a smile. He paused, and then continued, "If you insist, I have to sign your request as in NYC public employees rule. I know you didn't take your vacation last year. But there is too much work that needs doing now. Good statistics do not always reflect the reality."

"Unfortunately statistics have a clear political orientation," Jacob agreed.

"I'd like you, Jack, do me a favor and close the Pablo Rozario case," O'Burke said casually. "It would definitely improve the statistics of my division."

"It's nice of you, captain," Jacob said without enthusiasm. "That's a 'dead end' case, not a dream work." He stood up. "But I cannot refuse you," he grumbled on his way out.

"Dream and you'll be happy." O'Burke grinned, looking at Jacob's back.

After Jacob sat at his desk, he opened near empty folder and looked at the photo of a man on the first page. The disappearance of the undercover DEA agent Pablo Rozario really was a 'dead end' case. His body was never found, but Jacob had to prove it was murder and find a murderer. What did Jacob have at his disposal? Excepting Pablo's wife Josephine belief that her husband was murdered, Jacob had nothing. She hadn't the slightest idea that her husband was an undercover cop; rather she suspected him of being a drug dealer. They were separated on the eve of his death and Jacob, at the beginning of his investigation, even suspected that Josephine herself could be involved in her husband's death.

Jacob had discarded this version after he talked to Josephine. She told him that she had had a foggy vision of somebody's death; too foggy to be taken seriously. Jacob couldn't explain why he believed the woman. Something in her eyes told him that she had told the truth; something that couldn't be attached to the file.

This case was sent to the special homicide cases unit. Why didn't the DEA investigate the disappearance of one of its agents? Were they suspicious about someone from their staff?

Pablo had been going to meet someone from the Colombian Cartel in Holland. Why Holland? Pablo had dual citizenship, but it was only a formality. Josephine and Pablo spent their last vacation in Holland, in Amsterdam. Did he use his wife to create the image of an ordinary, married man? Why was the meeting scheduled in Holland? Soft drugs are legalized there. But Pablo investigated the drug supply to the U.S.; not soft drugs, heroin. Why did the man who intended to meet Pablo arrange the meeting in Holland? Why not in the U.S.? But Pablo wasn't killed in Holland. He had returned to the States safely. Who did he meet? And why he was killed here? There was no clue, Jacob thought tiredly.

Submerged in his thoughts, he put the file aside. To be an undercover DEA agent is a risky work. Jacob grinned as he remembered O'Burke's favorite words 'things happen.' Maybe it would be useful to fly to Amsterdam to meet Inspector Hence Vanbrunne of the Holland police force? But he had no definite idea to pursue there. Maybe it would also be useful to ask Josephine to fly out with him. She might be able to remember some places or people. But will he be able to persuade O'Burke to sigh a travel form? The captain doesn't like unpredictable expenses.

Jacob filled a travel form and went to O'Burke's office again.

"Captain," he said. "Several years ago Inspector Hence Vanbrunne of Holland police force investigated a murder case in the US that had involved a victim who had dual citizenship. I was assigned to that case also, and since then, we had kept a contact with Inspector Vanbrunne. Now I would like to talk to him about Pablo Rozario's case; never know who or what can give a hint."

"Dial his number," O'Burke retorted. "It's cheaper."

"A dry talk doesn't make the investigation faster," Jacob objected. Then he handed O'Burke the travel form to be approved. After O'Burke read it, he burst out laughing.

"You are kidding me, Jack," he said at last. "Suppose I can approve your travel expenses although you have no definite idea to pursue in Holland. But how can I approve the travel expenses for your companion who does not work in the NYPD?"

"Josephine is the only person who can help the investigation."

"No way, Jack. If you need a lady – travel companion, you can afford it at your own expense." O'Burke grinned ironically. Then he added, "You are a bachelor now."

"I can afford it," Jacob agreed, missing the irony.

Returning to his office, he called Josephine and asked her to fly out with him to Holland. When Josephine hesitated, he told her the trip would be at police expense, not his own, and then she agreed.

"Where did you stay in Amsterdam?" Jacob asked her.

"At the Hilton."

"Okay, Josephine," he said. "That's a good choice."

Then Jacob made a call and booked two rooms in the Amsterdam Hilton.

*

The transatlantic flight was calm, but Jacob didn't sleep. He couldn't sleep on a plane. When he was a kid and Moses took him to Israel for the first time, the Pan Am plane flew into a thunderstorm's epicenter. Jacob was so frightened by the cries of the people on board that since then he had been afraid of flying. If he could avoid it, he preferred any other type of transportation.

As soon as the plane reached its cruising altitude and the stewardesses supplied the passengers with a late meal, most of people on board fell asleep as if they were hypnotized when the main cabin lights were extinguished. Josephine was no exception. Jacob looked at her face carefully as if seeing the girl for the first time.

Jacob realized in that first moment of fully gazing upon

her, how faded every other female face must seem before her beauty. A strange sense of drowsiness began to steal over him. To discard it, he opened the small book his father had given him. He remembered Moses' words, 'You have to start with this thin book…' Jacob reread the title, *The Cabbalistic Treatise about Advantage and Disadvantage of Meal*, and again was surprised about the reason that his father advised him to start with it. He switched on the personal light and opened the book.

One of the greatest kabbalists Arizal said that abstinence from hametz during the Pesah holiday guarantees a man would be free from involuntary sin for a year. From voluntary sins, we cannot be secured because we possess the right of choice – if a man decides to do something bad, nothing will stop him. But involuntary violations, we do very often. When we had a Temple, there was a special sacrifice for the atonement of such sin. The fact of involuntary mistakes indicates that some internal defect is inside man. And to be secured from it, we have to get rid of hametz.

And the prohibition of hametz, and commandment to eat matza in Pesah concern the same meal. What makes hametz differ from matza? There is no principal difference. Matza is made from dough that didn't reach the phase of fermentation, hametz – from dough that has already reached fermentation.

We are what we eat – there is a close connection of this kind of meal with the highest level of our spiritual organization.

Jacob looked up from the page. That's why his father gave him the book – to tune him spiritually. Did he consider that Jacob's spiritual organization was at such a low level that he could not be involved in the investigation of Rabbi Lieberman's death? His father was right; it wasn't a matter of what meal Jacob ate. He looked at the face of the sleeping Josephine. She would never be worried about what kind of food was on her dinner table, he thought. Why do we Jews always complicate everything? Wouldn't the world be much better if Martin Luther's proposal about the unification of Judaism and Protestantism into one religion had been accepted by rabbis centuries ago? What prevented the unification? It was only such an 'insufficient item' as the laws of keeping kosher. But of course, it's not about meals; it's about Judaism. Jacob again concentrated on the text:

It is written that a man begins calling his parents 'papa' and 'mama' – 'aba' and 'ima' – only after he has tested grameneous plants. In some way, it adds to his awareness, developing it. There are two aspects here: calling for his biological parents, refers to hametz; calling for our God, our spiritual Father, refers to matza. Matza differs from hametz not by ingredients, but by a feature that seem to be symbolical: being made from dough that hadn't reached fermentation, symbolizing modesty. It's not an accident that matza is called the 'bread of poverty.' We begin the narration about Exodus with the words, "Here is the bread of poverty that our fathers ate in the land of Egypt." The roots of the words 'poverty' and 'modesty' are close: a poor man has no reasons to raise his "I" above others.

Think about the idea of Pesah's Seder. What we do during the Seder is unique. What are we telling our children? We do not boast about the military victories of our predecessors, what carefully keeps all other nations. Instead, we tell about our exodus from Egyptian slavery. Why? To diminish our ego and create the foundation of Judaism.

What kind of freedom did we gain when we left Egypt? Moses, when he went to the pharaoh, didn't revile the idea of slavery, but said, "Let my people go to serve God."

Somebody can ask the question: what kind of freedom is it — to be the slaves of God? But the idea of true freedom is in the fact that not any frames, or any forces, would dominate over man if he submits himself to God who is above all restrictions of the material world. But before accepting the power of The Highest Force, a man must diminish, if not remove, his own ego. This is an obligatory condition.

Jacob closed his eyes. *To remove his own ego...* Wasn't his life, just the contrary, a confirmation, inflammation of his ego? He persuaded himself that he had tried to find his own way in life, but was there a different way from the way of the Jewish people? He had found respect from other people, but did he find self-respect? *This is an obligatory condition...*

Jacob opened his eyes and looked at Josephine. Her eyes were open.

"It must be an interesting book if you read it instead of sleeping," she said. "What is it about?"

"About meals."

"Meals?" Her eyes widened with surprise. "Are you serious?"

"Yes, it's about what meals we can eat, and what we cannot," Jacob explained. Then he told her in simple words what was the difference between *matza* and *hametz*. "Rabbi Arizal wrote that *hametz* connects us with a very negative meaning – the possibility to be loaded by forces of evil – *Hitzonim*. Fulfilling the Torah's commandments, we attract God's light in our world; violating them, we animate forces of evil, giving them the opportunity to be fed from The Source."

"But if *hametz* is a poison feeding our egoism, and *matza* is a drug giving us the highest feeling, why not forbid the use of *hametz*?" Josephine asked.

"The difference between them has its principle meaning only during the Passover celebration, when we try to wake the Power of Absolute, the Power of the Creator, in ourselves," Jacob explained patiently.

Josephine gave him a strange glance. "It's too complicated for me," she said and closed her eyes again. Then she added, "You Jews are strange people."

"We are," Jacob agreed.

"Can I put my head on your shoulder?" she asked.

"Sure."

For some time he sat motionless, waiting until Josephine fell asleep. Then he again opened the book.

Matza and hametz are two levels, different in principle, of intellectual awareness. The first level corresponds with the category Chohma, the highest inner forces of our soul. Those inner forces of our soul can be divided into two levels: Sechel or forces of intellect, and Midot, forces of emotions.

Why do people put youth and beauty in the first place on the scale of human values? And only then, when both those meanings had gone, we try to compensate for them with knowledge. Jacob's thoughts continued to focus on the book's thoughts. But he felt he couldn't concentrate, and put the book off.

*

As the plane landed, it took them about an hour to pick

up their luggage; Josephine's suitcase was mistakenly placed on the other luggage track. At last they hired a taxi that delivered them to the Hilton.

Jacob noticed the door attendant examined them with hardly concealed curiosity. He probably thinks that Josephine's make-up is too bright for a woman accompanying a religious Jew, Jacob grinned to his thought.

They signed in, received their keys and went to their adjacent rooms. As soon as the bellhop delivered his bag, Jacob took a shower and put on the white robe hanging in the bathroom.

"Hilton is Hilton," he thought with satisfaction, picking up a fresh issue of *The Amsterdam News*.

Jacob took a bottle of beer from the room refrigerator, opened it, and sat in the chair. His glance stopped on the lithograph that hung on the wall. The charming atmosphere of a small Holland café inspired him, and he decided to invite Josephine to drink a cup of coffee with him. When the taxi dropped them off, he had noticed one of those open cafes across the street. He called her.

"Josephine, if you are alive after the flight, what about going out for a cup of coffee?" he asked.

"That would be nice. I'd just thought about the same thing, Jacob," she said.

He noticed that Josephine had called him 'Jacob.' Before, she had always called him 'Mr. Reterseil.'

*

They sat at a table, and a waitress brought them two small cups of coffee. Josephine glanced around.

"I like Holland since my childhood. Don't be surprised,

Jacob. I've been here several times with my mother. She was a singer, and once a year she was invited here to give concerts," she explained.

"What about your father?"

"He was jealous of every man who looked at her, so our family life wasn't too happy." Josephine lit a cigarette and sighed. "I almost don't remember my father. He died from a drug overdose when I was young," she said casually.

"That's a sad story," Jacob agreed. "I'm sorry."

Josephine managed a smile that seemed quite genuine.

"What about you?"

"I'm from a religious family; I am a Jew." A light smile touched the corners of Jacob's mouth.

"I guessed as much." She smiled in answer.

Then he turned to a matter that lay at the heart of his stay in Amsterdam.

"While here, with your husband, do you remember if he met anybody when you were present?" Jacob asked.

Josephine's face achieved something like a thoughtful look. Then she shook her head negatively.

"I am sorry to say not." Josephine looked simply at him.

"You were always together?"

"It was our vacation." She swallowed hard. Then she exclaimed, "Oh, maybe once… It was a spontaneous meeting. We were going out of the hotel when Pablo ran into a man who turned out to be his old acquaintance."

Jacob became animated. "An old acquaintance? Do you remember his name?"

"No, Pablo didn't introduce us. I didn't like him."

"Why?" Jacob asked carefully.

"He wasn't a gentleman. He said I was too pretty for Pablo."

"And how did Pablo react?"

"He smiled and said a man must be only a little bit more handsome than a monkey to make a woman happy; but he must have brains."

"And that's it? Then they parted?"

"That's it. The man gave Pablo his card and said, "It would be nice to have a chat with you, old chap. If you find the chance, call me.""

"Did Pablo call him?"

"I didn't hear him do it. I don't think so."

"Do you remember what the man looked like, Josephine?"

She closed her eyes, trying to recollect the face. Then she said, "No, he wore the typical face of a Scandinavian man. It was a plain face, like all faces around us."

"Why do you think he was a Scandinavian?"

"He spoke English with an accent."

"Wasn't it Spanish?"

Josephine offered him a thin smile. "Believe me, not." She closed her eyes again, and then glanced at Joseph. "I remembered he shook his head like he had a nervous tick."

Jacob took a big, strong breath deep in his chest, feeling a moment of relaxed satisfaction. He had not taken Josephine to Amsterdam in vain. Then he said, "I think your recollection will be very useful for me."

Josephine nodded silently. Jacob thought their conversation looked more like an interrogation, not a friendly chat. He had stopped asking her questions.

"I hope you'll enjoy your stay in Amsterdam," Jacob said. "The city has the charm of old European cities. I feel as if I were born here." He smiled. "My predecessors were from

Hungary; not too far from here, using the European scale," Jacob explained.

"This trip isn't a vacation for me, Jacob," Josephine said thoughtfully. "But it would be nice if you invite me to dinner before us return home. Do you promise?" She crossed her arms and looked away.

"I definitely do, Josephine," he said warmly.

6.

Inspector of Criminal Police Hence Vanbrunne was a huge man, six and a half feet tall, broad in proportion. Five years previously, while working with the Interpol, he had been the lead investigator on the murder of a notorious Holland politician who was closely connected to extremist Muslim groups. The suspect had flown to the U.S., and when the Amsterdam police asked NYPD for assistance, Jacob was assigned to help Hence Vanbrunne. Since then both detectives had maintained a friendly relationship.

When Jacob called Hence at his office, the man didn't sound very surprised.

"Hi, Jack," Hence said as if they had seen each other just a few days ago. "What's new in New York? Police headquarters is still at the same place?"

"All's the same, Hence. Only the mayors have changed and the police commissioners. But our job doesn't depend on them."

"When are you going to visit old Europe, Jack? It would be nice to have lunch together," Hence said diplomatically.

"I hear you, Hence!" Jacob laughed. "I'm already in Amsterdam, not far from you."

"Something urgent? In such a case, come to my office," Hence offered.

"No, thanks. I would call my visit to Holland semi-official. But it would be nice if you could give me a peace of advice on one matter."

"I am at your disposal, Jack. What about having lunch at 'Mother's Kitchen'? It's a restaurant in the harbor. Every cab driver in town can deliver you to that restaurant without any problem."

"That's a go!"

"I'll be waiting for you at five o'clock," Hence clarified and hung up.

*

When Jacob told the cab driver the name of the restaurant, the driver didn't hesitate and set off toward the harbor. Not too far from the gate to the dock, the car stopped.

"It's one-way street, sir," the cabdriver said. "The restaurant is behind the corner."

"Okay." Jacob paid for the ride and got out.

Looking around, he saw a line of warehouses stretched for over half a mile to the left, and above their roofs, the masts of ships and the jibs of cranes pointed to the sky like skeletal fingers. It's not a nice place for a famous restaurant, he thought. But when Jacob turned round the corner, he has changed his mind. The restaurant was on the other side, overlooking the sea and open to a wonderful, fantastic view of the ancient castle debris.

Both police officers were punctual men; at five o' clock sharp they shook hands near the restaurant entrance.

Hence asked for a private table, one situated near the glass wall where they could enjoy the sunset. The sun was falling beyond the horizon, diving into the sea, but the sun's rays reflecting from the sea's surface, created a magnificent, surreal picture. The pattern was so beautiful that Jacob kept silent until the sun finally disappeared. The horizon became gray as if the many-colored, magnificent picture had never existed.

The restaurant was really good. The menu choices were vast and the food tasty and succulent. Even the Turkish coffee that arrived after they finished their meals couldn't have been better if they had drunk it somewhere in Lebanon. While they enjoyed their meals, Hence asked no questions. He was a typical Scandinavian man, reserved and reliable.

At last Jacob wiped his lips. He lit a cigarette and thought that the NY cigarette ban was more political than a medical achievement.

"The reason I called you, Hence, is not trivial. I have to close a case, but I haven't the slightest idea how to start working on it," Jacob said frankly. Then he told briefly about the case.

He decided not to mention Rabbi Lieberman's death or his father's suggestion that in that case there was an attempt of a soul transfusion. It would be too much for such a good, righteous Christian as Hence Vanbrunne. And in any case, it had no connection to Josephine's husband's death.

"The only information I have is Josephine's statement that she had a vague vision of her husband's death," Jacob said. He clucked his tongue unhappily.

Hence's eyebrow rose in surprise.

"A foggy vision cannot be used in the police work," he agreed with a difficult smile.

"This girl and her husband had spent a vacation week here on the eve of his disappearance in the U.S. In any case I brought her with me. She remembered only a brief meeting in the streets, but she gave me a description of the man. Maybe it was a casual meeting," Jacob said doubtfully.

When he gave Hence the man's description, Hence thought a little.

"Frankly, I cannot recollect such a man among our officers," he said, and took a deep, fortifying gulp of air. "But I'll check, Jack."

"Maybe in the narcotics division," Jacob suggested thoughtfully.

"That division is small here. Since Holland had legalized soft drugs, we don't have big problems in that field. Anyone who wants 'to fly to another world,' can use soft drugs. That's why big drug dealers avoid Holland; too small profits and too risky to deliver heroin. The traffic from Russia goes to the U.S. bypassing us. I think one day American politicians will also come to the same conclusion that we did: prohibition doesn't work. It only pumps billions of dollars into the pockets of dealers. It's much more reasonable to pump that money into the state budget," Hence said. He strongly supported the idea of drug legalization.

"They're taking care of the 'public's health,' Hence." Jacob grinned. "Our DEA has a budget comparable to the Pentagon's, and hundred of thousands employees. If you fire the entire army, do you think they'd be happy? It's only business, Hence; in our country, it's only business. Nobody's interested to stop the war on drugs." He sighed and ordered another cup of coffee.

"I don't have a clue about how I can be useful to you," Hence considered thoughtfully. "Maybe it makes sense that you to talk to a lady, Madam Wong by name. She owns a body treatment salon here in Amsterdam."

"A body salon?" Jacob didn't sound convinced.

"I said, 'a body treatment salon,'" Hence said, smiling. "You can receive there a Swedish massage for your body, and also an opium massage for your soul. It's illegal, of course, but we close our eyes because she supplies us with information we need. Not talking about the fact that we know all her customers." Hence took a pen from his pocket and wrote down the address. "It's not far away from the hotel where you stay."

"Can I mention your name, Hence?"

"Sure you can. Tell Madam Wong 'best regards from big boy Hence.'"

Neither detective discussed business after that – they enjoyed the meal, the peaceful night sounds, and the satisfaction of having completed another day's work. A pleasant breeze blew, and the night was blazing with stars when they wished each other good night.

*

Getting settled for the night, Jacob heard a knock at his hotel room door.

"May I come in? I feel so lonely, Jacob" Josephine asked, standing on the threshold.

"Sure, I just had a meeting with Inspector Vanbrunne," Jacob informed her, and felt confusion rising in him against his will.

Josephine sat down and crossed her hands over her chest. Then she shot him a wide-eyed glance.

"Please," she said in deep voice, "don't leave me alone next time. Take me with you."

"I promise," Jacob replied defensively.

"Bye now, Jacob." She stood up, moving to the door. On the threshold, Josephine turned back. Her eyes registered a moment of confusion on Jacob's face.

7.

The next day, as he promised, Jacob and Josephine had breakfast together followed by a trip to Madam Wong's salon.

When Jacob stopped a cab and told the driver the address, he looked at the couple with a raised brow.

"You're kidding me, sir," he said. "It's just around the corner."

It was Jacob's turn to be surprised as he couldn't have imagined that such a 'salon' would be situated in the center of the city.

Presently they came to a wide, wooden door set in the wall of a beautifully decorated building. The red sign beside the door contained some Chinese characters painted in black. Jacob tugged the bell and, after a minute, an old Oriental man opened the door. He bowed to Jacob and Josephine, and then silently stood aside as they entered.

Jacob looked around. They were in a hall lined with painted wallpaper. Lustrous red lacquer covered all the wood trims. Ornate lanterns hung from the ceiling. He felt a sweet smell in the air.

As the old man quietly stood nearby, Jacob said, turning to him, "Tell Madam Wong, please, that a friend of 'big boy Hence' would like to talk to her."

Without a word, the old man bowed and left. Soon he returned with a Chinese woman dressed in a richly embroidered, dark-red robe. Her dark hair was pinned up. She wore black silk trousers under her robe, and red slippers on her tiny feet. Looking at her pleasant face, Jacob thought that, under no circumstances, she could be called a manager of a 'narcotics salon.'

"Hi," the woman said, bowing. "I am happy to see a friend of big boy Hence at my place." Madam Wong gestured toward an inner room. "Please consent to enter my place of business." Her voice was low and musical, and her English was quite without accent although her 'hi' sounded more Chinese than English. "A friend of my friend is a friend of mine," she said smiling. "I have been honored with big boy Hence's friendship," she explained.

While Jacob explained Madam Wong who he and Josephine were and what he wanted, Josephine looked around. The light was very dim; only two or three Chinese lanterns penetrated the smoky darkness. Everything in the room that could be painted or lacquered was the same deep blood red. The door posts were carved with curling, snarling dragons painted gold. Visitors tended to get a sense of oppressive richness as the room seemed to have taken on the shape of the collective dreams of all those who had ever gone there to seek oblivion.

Jacob and Madam Wong were speaking in low voices behind Josephine. Looking for somewhere to sit, Josephine saw a coach standing near the wall candle. She wanted to reach the coach, but felt dizzy. The light smoke drifted up from the candles hanging on the walls, leaving her enticing and curious. She felt as it wasn't enough air for her and inhaled deeper; once, then again, and…suddenly darkness came to her, with stifling heat.

Josephine found herself lying on the floor, near the coach, with her eyes wide open searching the darkness. A convulsive fear squeezed her heart. She tried to move, but could not; her limbs were too weak for the slightest motion.

Then Josephine felt an awful fear penetrated every cell of her body. Her heart thumped in panic against her ribs. And then the scream ripped through the darkness like a sharp sword. She thought she would die from fear. Then she heard voices.

"Where is it?"

"Not with me!"

"They are coming. Be quick!"

Then Josephine heard the hideous sound of a sharp instrument sinking into meat – a sort of tearing noise, followed by a gasp and groan as if the air had been forced out of a man's lungs all at once. That splashing sound had quickly died away into a trickle.

A tiny spark of light had reached Josephine. But she couldn't escape the bad dream. She knew what was coming next: a man's voice –

"Look! Look at me! You are not dead yet…"

It was an unfamiliar for her voice, a voice she couldn't recognize. And she couldn't see the man's face; it was too dark.

This was the point where Josephine had always woken up before. But now something else happened. The light came closer to her and was held to one side. A man's face looked down at her.

53

Josephine was again awash with fear. She was almost mad with it. She thought, "*I am going to die… He will kill me like he has just killed Pablo…*"

Suddenly she felt a sharp blow on her cheek. Josephine heard the sound of it a second later. Everything was still dark around her, but the next blow on her cheek helped her to regain consciousness. Josephine was awake, her face streaming with tears. She took a deep breath that failed to soothe her frayed nerves. She opened her eyes.

Jacob was standing beside her. Without thinking, she flung her arms around his neck and sobbed. He held her tightly, saying nothing. Madam Wong stood a short distance to the side, watching Josephine closely. When she saw that Josephine was conscious again, she stepped forward and bowed.

"Please rest, Ms. Josephine," she said, handing Josephine a glass of water.

"What happened?" Josephine asked weakly. Her lips and tongue didn't seem to be functioning properly.

"You were affected by the smoke," Jacob explained. "You must have inhaled more than you thought." Then Jacob turned to Madam Wong. "But to go under all at once – isn't that very unusual, Madam Wong?"

"This is not Ms. Josephine's first encounter with that smoke," she explained.

"I've never smoked opium in my life," Josephine objected weakly, turning her deep black eyes on Jacob.

"It distresses me to contradict you, Ms. Josephine, but you have breathed the smoke before. It's my business, I know," she said casually, but her lips tightened in a grin. "What did you see in your vision?"

"I saw the scene that has come to me many times. It was

like a nightmare, a bad dream. I saw my husband being killed, and the man who had killed him. I've seen the man's face; he was too close to me. I am not crazy!"

"You are not, Ms. Josephine," Madam Wong said, trying to sound encouraging. "You were under the influence of opium. Its power is unbounded. It hides secrets of the past so well that the sharpest eyes in brightest daylight would never find them. And then it reveals them like buried and forgotten treasure. What you had seen, Ms. Josephine, is a mental memory, not a dream," Madam Wong said firmly.

"Did you recognize the man?" Jacob couldn't hide his excitement.

"It was the man that we had met near the hotel entrance – the man with the nervous tick in his neck," Josephine said weakly.

"Is that possible, Madam Wong, to see the scene you have never seen before physically?" Jacob asked in surprise.

"It is," Madam Wong remarked shortly.

"Do you really mean to say that Josephine's been under the influence of opium before, and that this nightmare of hers is a mental memory of the awful time when her husband was killed?" Jacob re-asked again.

"It's possible, Mr. Reterseil. It is what happened now. I can see plainly what is invisible to you, just as a doctor can see plainly what is troubling his patient," Madam Wong explained.

Josephine felt the urge to weep again. "But I have never smoked opium, trust me," she said, turning to Jacob. "I am drug free."

"You have taken it twice, Ms. Josephine, believe me," Madam Wong said, turning to her. "Maybe the first time it was in your childhood, and you didn't remember; but it had happened."

"Our visit to your salon, Madam Wong, turned out to be very useful for us." Jacob bowed to Madam Wong. "Now it's high time for us to tell you good-bye and to thank you."

"Maybe, Mr. Reterseil, you and Ms. Josephine want to receive not a soul but a body treatment? We provide the best Swedish massage in the city," Madam Wong offered.

"I think it would be too much for Josephine; and for me too." Jacob smiled. "We wish you the best, Madam Wong," he added.

"My best regards to big boy Hence," she said as Jacob and Josephine were heading to the door.

Outside it was a bright, sunny day. Josephine welcomed the fresh air, and she inhaled deeply. She found soon that the pounding in her head diminished a little, but she still felt dizzy and her back was wet with perspiration. Jacob waved to a taxi, and the ride soon made the opium den seem like a dream itself.

They hadn't spoken in the car; Jacob seemed to know when she wanted silence. Only when she opened her door, did Josephine turn to him and said softly, "You can trust me, Jacob. It was the man with a nervous tick, who had killed Pablo." Weariness was starting to show in her eyes.

Josephine went inside her room and began to close the door, but Jacob followed her.

"You are too weak to be alone today," he said softly. His strong eyes were full of rare tenderness. "You surely know, Josephine, that death is not the end of all existence. Every fiber of my being tells me that death doesn't end all."

She glanced at him gratefully, but her face twisted in revulsion.

"It's still daytime. You need to take a nap; but this evening, I invite you to have dinner with me if you don't mind accompanying such an old man." Jacob's lips turned up in a smile.

"It would be great," Josephine said frankly, her voice was energized.

Josephine lay on the sofa. Heat flooded her as her mind called up the recent memories she just hadn't been able to shake, no matter how hard she tried. At last she fell asleep. Jacob covered her by a plaid blanket and left, quietly closing the door behind him.

*

Returning to his room, Jacob called Hence Vanbrunne.

"I have news for you, Hence," he said. Then Jacob told him what had happened in Madam Wong's salon. "Josephine identified the man who killed her husband. He turned out to be the same man with the nervous tick in his neck, whom she and her husband had met near the hotel. It was an awful experience for the poor girl," Jacob said, summing up.

"I also have news, Jack," Hence said, "good and bad. Which do you want first?"

"I always like the good one first. It'll raise my spirits high enough so I'm not in a bad mood when I hear the bad news." Jacob smiled.

"Okay. The good news is that we have identified the man with the tick. He turned out to be an undercover detective in the narcotic division. That's why I hadn't seen him around headquarters; he's a rare visitor. Did that news raise your mood, Jack?"

"It definitely did!"

"The bad news is that we have no evidence against him." Hence paused. "Maybe except for one thing; he's too rich for an undercover officer. But it's not a crime."

"To be rich isn't a crime," Jacob agreed. "Did you check if he had been in the U.S. at the time that Pablo Gonzales had vanished?"

"We did. He'd been in the U.S.; it was his vacation. I have put him under the glass bell, Jack, and think it's only a matter of time until we catch him," Hence reassured him.

"It's only a matter of time," Jacob agreed. "Our entire life, Hence, is a matter of time." Then he changed the topic. "I'm very grateful to you, Hence, for the help, and I do hope to see you in the U.S. one day."

Jacob heard in the receiver Hence's laughter. "It's not likely to expect me in the near future, Jack," he said. "Crime in Holland is negligible, and it's hard to justify being sent out of the country on a business trip. Regarding to my vacations, I love Old Europe."

"You never know. But it would be my pleasure, Hence. Take care." Jacob hung up.

He went downstairs to the bar to have a drink and to think over his report to Captain O'Burke. Closing the Pablo Rozario case, he'd be able to concentrate on the investigation of Rabbi Lieberman's death. In his thoughts, more and more often, Jacob began to consider it the most important investigation in his career.

Not in my career; that's the wrong word, he thought; rather, in my life.

*

Josephine has called him about six o'clock. "Did you forget, Jacob, that you'd invited me to dinner?"

"It would be impossible to forget that, Josephine. It's not every evening that I invite such a beautiful lady as you," Jacob joked. "I'll meet you downstairs in half an hour."

When Jacob arrived downstairs, he saw that his words were not just a polite compliment. His mouth hung open as he flashed a quick, wondering glance at Josephine. She was tall and attractive. Her eyes, black as night, were huge and wide. Her hair was mess of curls. She looked like she knew that she was a creature of light; and she wanted to stay that way, a creature of light in a world of mud.

Having seen Jacob, Josephine smiled openly at him.

"It's a lovely evening, isn't it? Where we are going?"

"I have no idea." Jacob shrugged. "It's my first visit to Amsterdam."

"Then let's choose a restaurant at random," Josephine offered. "Let's go to the left, then turn to the right, and again to the left; and we'll enter the first restaurant we see, okay? We're in the center of the city; I suppose all the restaurants here are good."

After they passed a couple of streets, they saw a restaurant sign that read "Ulenshpigel."

The name sounds familiar, Jacob thought.

It reminded him of a book he had read in his childhood. What it was about? Jacob had forgotten the book's plot, but remembered that the father of the main protagonist, Til Ulenshpigel, had met his death in a bonfire, struggling for Holland independence from Spain, and 'his ash knocked at his son's heart.'

As they went in, Jacob thought that Josephine perhaps had already been in this place and had not chosen it at random.

The restaurant was small and cozy. It would be difficult to find the better place for a quiet dinner. Sitting at table, Jacob observed that the light revealed a rare softness and refinement in Josephine's face. The expression on her face had changed since they were in Madam Wong's salon. It seemed to Jacob that all heaven of God's indwelling pardon, love and peace had come to dwell with her.

As a waiter took their orders, Jacob looked around. A pianist on a stage was playing a half-forgotten melody. Josephine's sparkling eyes in front of him led Jacob's thoughts far away from the murder case that brought him to Holland.

"You are beautiful, Josephine," Jacob said frankly.

"Thank you, Jacob," she said and laughed. "I'm happy you've seen me at last!"

Waiting for an appetizer, Jacob told Josephine about his last telephone conversation with Hence Vanbrunne.

"He promised to get this guy and, believe me, he will," Jacob reassured her.

"You know, Jacob," Josephine said thoughtfully, "I don't understand how people can kill other people and not be afraid of God's punishment."

"'Do not kill' is not the only commandment that people violate," Jacob remarked. "Regarding the fear of punishment… All criminals hope to avoid it; that's human nature."

"Let's not to talk about fear," she said softly.

"Okay. Tell me about yourself."

"There's nothing interesting." Josephine smiled. "I was born, went to school, then to college, then I was married." She paused. "For half a year," she added.

"What's your profession?"

"I am a speech pathologist, "Josephine explained. "I work with kids."

"It's a great profession for a woman," Jacob agreed. "Why did you choose it?"

"In childhood, I had a problem pronouncing several sounds, and my schoolmates teased me. So I decided to help kids who have the same problem."

"You are a good person, Josephine."

"I am a Catholic girl; we trust in God."

"Yes, we trust in God," Jacob agreed.

"May I ask you a serious question, Jacob?" she asked, turning her deep eyes to him.

"Sure."

"If we trust in one God, why do Jews hate Christians?"

Jacob burst out laughing. His laughter was long and sincere. Then he wiped away the tears that had appeared in his eyes.

"Dear girl, it's just the opposite. Some Christians hate Jews. Our problem is that we Jews cannot hate. If we could hate, the world would be a much better place."

"But why do you think that Christians hate Jews?" Josephine insisted.

"I think Judaism and Christianity, over the years, became different religions," Jacob said thoughtfully.

"We trust in the same God. What's the difference?"

"This is a rather strange conversation for a farewell dinner, isn't it?" Jacob smiled. "To talk about religion when such a beautiful lady is near me..."

He tried to change the topic, but Josephine returned him to the same point.

"Please, Jacob, explain what's the difference?"

"It's not easy to explain it in words, Josephine, but I'll try," he said thoughtfully. "Christianity and all other religions in the world are men-made; Judaism is the only one given by God."

"Why do you call Christianity a man-made religion?" she asked with sufficient vehemence, and gazed at him wide-eyed. She found herself wondering.

"Look, a Jew named Jesus was killed by Romans two millennia ago. He was a good man, like many others. But only a hundred years later, another Jew named Saul – you know him as Saint Paul – called Jesus a messenger of God and created Christianity. By the way, at the end of his life, Saul asked Sanhedrin to forgive his sin – he had realized that his attempt to revise God's religion was the biggest blunder of his life."

Josephine listened to Jacob very attentively.

"I never heard anything about this from my priest," she said frankly. "I know that Judaism is the base of Christianity."

Josephine gave him a confidant, knowing smile. She was a clever woman, and she was trying to build a bridge between her and Jacob.

"You are right, my dear girl," Jacob agreed.

"But what's the difference?"

"I think I can formulate it in one sentence." Jacob smiled. "In Judaism you can do everything that you want to do except what is prohibited; in Christianity everything is prohibited except what you are allowed to do," he finally responded as he saw a flicker of understanding in her face.

Josephine laughed. "Jacob, you are a sage; you're the first sage I've ever met. And I thank Lord for meeting you," she said seriously.

The dinner arrived and they stopped discussing serious matters. Half an hour later the small restaurant was full. A violinist had joined the pianist on the stage, and Josephine asked, "Will you dance with me, Jacob, please?"

"I am not much a dancer," he tried to joke, but she was insistent. "Please, just one dance."

They went to the empty space on the floor near the stage. Jacob lightly embraced her body and closed his eyes. He shivered and was happy when the music stopped.

"I am not much a dancer," he repeated.

"It's a matter of practice." Josephine smiled. A smile lit up her face, and Jacob thought she was beautiful.

Youth is always beautiful, he thought. It's a matter of time; my time has gone. He smiled to his thoughts.

"What are you smiling at?" she asked, searching his face.

"I – I can't tell you exactly. It's just a feeling."

"A feeling of what?"

"I feel that we can take nothing for granted. We now have only good days or great days. This is a feeling about our preparation for life."

"The best way to prepare for life is to begin to live," Josephine said, and Jacob again thought she was a clever woman. Since Josephine had so obviously suffered since her husband was killed, all he wanted to do was to make her well again.

When they returned to the hotel and he was about wishing her good night, Jacob said, "It was a lovely evening, wasn't it?"

"One of the best in my life," Josephine agreed.

The door to her room closed.

*

When Jacob was in the bed, he saw in a flash what had

happened in the last two days. His mind trailed off to the scene at Madam Wong's salon, every item of it seen in a new, vivid light. He had finally realized that his idea of drugs being involved in the mystery of *Zohar* creation was naïve, if not stupid.

I can't sleep, he murmured, remembering the book.

His fingers sought the electric switch. Getting out of bed, he found the book and went back to bed. Lying on his elbow, he opened to the page he had last read, but suddenly saw Josephine in the doorway. She came in and sat on the bed.

"Please, Jacob, make me warm," she whispered, switching the light off. "I cannot sleep. I keep seeing the killer behind my eyes." Her voice was trembling as she was overcome with emotions.

"Josephine, I cannot take the advantage of my position," he whispered, still trying to resist.

Jacob felt his body tremble. Since he had divorced Gwendolyn more than a year ago, he had not experienced a woman's tenderness.

"You won't," Josephine whispered in answer, and closed Jacob's mouth with her kiss, forcing him to forget about everything…

8.

In the plane on the way home, Jacob opened the book again.

The inner forces of our soul can be divided into two levels: Sechel or the forces of intellect, and Midot, the forces of emotions. In turn, Sechel consists of three forces marked by the abbreviation CHABAD: Hohma, Bina and Daat. The word Hohma is translated as "wisdom", but in reality, it is only the first splash of our awareness. Awareness does not exist yet; and then, suddenly – eureka! A man still cannot explain what he had caught, even to himself; it's only a splash of light he had seen at a level that was beyond his understanding. Hohma, as a force of the soul, is the main spherot of the highest world Atzilut where "I" does not exist.

The next level is the level of understanding. On this level, the main factor is man himself. I understand with my brain, with my logic. It's a lower level, and to this point, it is only a reflection of Hohma's light.

The level where the man feels himself to be God's creation is the level BINA. It's the base of the world BRIA, the first of the created worlds.

Jacob closed his eyes. That was the reason his father, a sage, had given him the book. He wanted to open Jacob's eyes to the first splash of awareness, to show what was beyond Jacob's understanding. He returned to the text again, and read on with a strange, breathless interest, with a sudden sense of hush upon him:

As per Kabbalah, the letter 'heh' corresponds to the spherot Malchut, the lowest of the ten spherots. It consists of three rays, which mark all nine spherots above. They are divided into three layers. The highest layer corresponds to the horizontal ray, - it's HABAD (HOHMA, BINA and DAAT.) Next two levels cor- responding to vertical rays are HESED, GVURA, TIFERET, NETZAH, HOD, IESOD.

The gap under the horizontal ray means afflux of light into MALCHUT from the spherot HOHMA. This kind of lighten- ing is the total absence of ego, absence of "I."

Jacob paused in his reading, and closed his eyes. His face, as he lay down the book, reflected a strange new perplexity. He remembered the letter *'alef'* on the Rabbi Lieberman's chest. What did it mean? If it were the letter *'heh,'* it would be considered a proof of the absence of the rabbi's ego. But what did it mean *'alef'*? Was it a sign that the rabbi was on his way to the world *Atzilut*?

At length, he gave up on the perplexing attempt to think out a solution to the mystery of Rabbi Lieberman's death, telling himself that with the coming of a new day, he would begin a definite search for the real facts of this great mystery.

With an exercise of will, Jacob settled himself and avoided thinking about it. Instead, he looked at Josephine, studying her face for a moment. She was sitting quietly, looking out the window. What was she thinking about? Was she real or a product of my imagination? He grinned at the thought. He tried to have a nap and think about nothing. But in his short night dream, he saw Josephine pointing out to the letter *alef* on the Rabbi Lieberman's chest, and asking him a question what it meant. There is something wrong with my mind now that there wasn't before, Jacob thought, opening his eyes.

When the plane landed and they were waiting for a taxi, Josephine turned to him.

"I know you won't call me, Jacob," she said, pushing back a sprig of hair. "There are things that I've experienced and I cannot explain. But I want you to know that meeting you has changed my life. I will never be able to hate anybody." Josephine paused and added, "Especially Jews." She kissed Jacob on the cheek. "Thank you for everything," she said warmly.

"Be happy, Josephine. Happiness is where we find it, but rarely where we seek it. Thanks to you, I understood that little moments make our life huge. God bless you," Jacob said, forcing himself to look at her eyes. What he read in her eyes was pain. Understanding he had been speaking intently, he stopped talking and gave her a hug.

Josephine jumped in a taxi that had just swerved to the curb beside them. In the next moment, the taxi disappeared around the corner.

*

Captain O'Burke had just read the report when Jacob arrived at his office. He put the papers down and looked at Jacob. He liked the report, and brightened a bit at seeing Jacob.

"When I sent you to Holland, Jack, I was ready to eat my hat that you would fail to solve this particular case, and I have approved the useless traveling expenses," he said in a pleasant enough voice.

"I couldn't fail, captain, as I was eager to receive my long-awaited vacation." Jacob smiled, seemingly unaffected by the captain's pleasant tone.

"You deserve it, Jack." O'Burke handed him a piece of paper. "I've signed your annual leave request. I think it's even better that you not to be in the office right now."

Picking up the paper, Jacob looked at the captain questioningly.

"If you have ruined 'Princess of Harlem's' career, it could cost our mayor his reelection," O'Burke explained. "So there will be a wide search for a scapegoat." Then he smiled broadly. "At any case, it was worth punishing this untouchable bitch."

"Punishment isn't my business," Jacob muttered on his way out.

That Jew is incredible, Captain O'Burke thought as Jacob left. I think it's high time to promote him to a chief inspector position. But would a promotion have any effect on his life?

9.

Now Jacob could concentrate on what he considered the most important task before him. If he were asked why he considered it so important, he couldn't answer. Rabbi Lieberman's death was an enigma, but why did God lead Jacob to solving this enigma? Was it so important to know who took part in that attempt of transfusion of a soul? It was God's will, as everything that happens: life and death, love and hatred, justice and injustice, dreams and disappointments. Everything. Jacob's thoughts were hectic and indefinite.

Why was it he who had touched the enigma? If Captain O'Burke hadn't asked him to go to the Kings County Hospital, he would have remained, as before, Inspector Reterseil, a good cop doing a good job.

Now he is another man who obsessed with his wish to find 'the wizard of our generation' as his father called the man. What would change if he had found this man? Nothing. Could Jacob expect the man to confess to involuntarily manslaughter? Nonsense. It would be impossible to prove his guilt, just as it wasn't possible to prove Pablo Rozario's murder. Even if Hence Vanbrunne arrested the man who killed Pablo, the man wouldn't be as stupid as to confess to a murder committed in the U.S., and to be extradited for trial. It was a dead case, inevitable damage in the war on drugs. Unfortunately for Jacob, in this case it was not the moral satisfaction for him of naming the murderer. It had changed nothing; just as nothing would be changed when he had found the man who was involved in that soul transfusion. But in such a case, why were all his thoughts concentrated only in one direction – to find the mysterious wizard?

Jacob began his work by analyzing the computer information he had received from Abe Berger. When Jacob opened the file, his mood plummeted – it consisted of hundreds and hundreds of names and addresses. To find the one that he searched for was like finding a tiny grain of gold in the mass of sand. But he had to find it.

Jacob began classifying the list by frequency of visits. He separated groups of people who had visited Rabbi Lieberman's home twice, thrice and more. Then he looked for people who had visited Rabbi Lieberman frequently for the last six months before his death. And at last Jacob highlighted several names that attracted his attention.

It would be Sezeuph's work if Jacob hadn't had access to the main police computer. Opening police files, Jacob received the extremely confidential information. He was surprised at how many years this information was kept in the police bank of files. What for purpose? Some information had made him nauseous. He considered Jews better than other people. But among them he saw thieves and sexual maniacs, crooks and adulterers. They were no better than any of the others; they were like them.

But most of people who had visited Rabbi Lieberman's home were not, of course, found in police records. They were ordinary people, with their ordinary problems. What problems did they carry to the rabbi's attention? Were their problems worth the rabbi's attention? Only they and late Rabbi Lieberman knew it.

But the harder Jacob struggled to achieve his goal – to find the man who caused Rabbi Lieberman's death – the more difficulty he had overcoming it, difficulty caused, at least in part, by the strain of his effort.

"You try too hard. Relax, take it easy and try again," he told himself. "You should never try to force results. At any case, I'll find the man."

Jacob felt that being so tired changed his optimism, and caught the thought that his attempts to persuade himself about his search's success looked like self-hypnoses.

Jacob awarded himself half a day of relaxation.

"Charley, what do you think if we'll go for a walk?" he asked the dog, and heard his happy barking in answering. Charley definitely understood the question and waved with his tail, waiting obediently near the entrance door while Jacob found a leash.

When they went out, Jacob felt almost intoxicated by the blue sky and fresh air. He looked at the sky and tried to form some pattern from the light clouds on the sky. He always did it when wanted to be relaxed, but that day might show form no patterns at all.

"We'll find him, Charley," he said aloud to better convince himself. Having heard his name, the dog barked in answer.

Charley and Jacob walked down the street in the direction of the park.

The night's light rain had given way to a warm, slightly misty day. New York looked wan, like a convalescent after a drunken night. Although Jacob held Charley's leash, the dog ran far in front of him, constantly looking back as if he wanted to be assured that Jacob was still there, not the dog walker.

When they reached the park, Jacob sat on a bench. Everything was eerily still and silent. The calm suited his mood.

He hadn't walked Charley for a long time. Cruel! He had given his dog to a dog walker's care and thought it was the same. Charley needed him. Jacob glanced at Charley, and it seemed that he saw sparks of happiness in the dog's eyes. He leaned over to pet the dog tenderly. Only in America, Jacob grinned, was there such an occupation as dog walker. Dog owners are too busy to pay attention or time to their pets. Why did they, in that case, adopt a dog?

Looking around, Jacob saw a black woman-babysitter with five children. The babysitter didn't look any different from the dog walker. When they came closer, Jacob saw that all the children belonged to different racial groups. He guessed that the kids had been adopted by one of the so-called celebrities, for whom the kids' adoption was no different from pets' adoption. "Only in America," Jacob said aloud, and thought that such 'adoption' was no better than child abuse.

Jacob and Charley walked until Jacob's legs began to ache. Even Charley looked exhausted and could hardly move, this time lagging far behind Jacob. Then Jacob flagged down a taxi and returned home. His thoughts were again concentrating on the mysterious case he had to resolve.

*

Even with access to the main police computer, the work took Jacob almost two weeks before he finalized the list of

Rabbi Lieberman's most frequent visitors. Two of them were not in the police files, the third was.

Obviously in the past, all of them had had strong reasons to wish their own souls to be purified. But only one of them was the person that Jacob needed to ask the question about what had happened that night in Rabbi Lieberman's house.

10.

The first of the three most frequent of Rabbi Lieberman's visitors was Aaron Fisher, the only man with a police record.

Jacob looked at the photo on the first page of the file. It had been taken more than twenty years previously when the man was about sixty years old. He had an ascetic face. His thin hair was white. Each eyebrow looked like giant, fuzzy, white caterpillar perched above his eye, dramatic in contrast to his skin. His sad eyes attracted Jacob; maybe they were sadder than the usual sorrowful Jewish eyes. The more Jacob looked at Aaron Fisher's face, the more he realized it wasn't normal Jewish sadness that attracted him. Rather it was a painful sadness. The man couldn't hide it behind the oversize glasses that he wore.

Aaron Fisher was a successful businessman, a self-made millionaire, the owner of a shoe store chain. He was also a lavish philanthropist and the head of a large family: his son, a Harvard graduate, was an assemblyman from Manhattan; his daughter was a doctor; there were four grandchildren.

Why had this information been kept in police records

for more than twenty years? Neither Aaron Fisher nor any of members of his family had problems with the law; they didn't even have any unpaid traffic tickets. Nothing at all, Jacob thought and opened the next page.

The file was created in the nineteen eighty and was based on an anonymous report. When Jacob read it, he felt a shiver had passed over his body.

The anonymous informer had said that in 1944, at the age of sixteen, Aaron Fisher had killed his twin-brother and became a capo in the Nazi concentration camp. He personally selected children to be killed by the Polish guards.

The report contained breathtaking information about what had happened in 1944. The anonymous informant had written: "It was a small concentration camp for Jewish children between six and seventeen years old. The commandant of the camp, Scharfuhrer SS Fritz Bruchner, was a pedophile and a sadist. As the result of a serious wound he had received on the Western front, he had lost an eye and his right hand. As he couldn't go back to his full duties, he was appointed a commandant of a small concentration camp for Jewish children. It was a special camp supplying 'live material' for SS medical research.

Scharfuhrer Bruchner was the only German officer; the rest of the guards were the Poles; but their pathological anti-Semitism was no less strong than Bruchner's.

The concentration camp was located in a small, provincial Polish town called Ruzniki, still far from war intersections. Life there was boring, and when Scharfuhrer Bruchner was tired of heavy drinking, he amused himself by killing Jewish children.

One day he ordered two recently admitted twin boys to stand in front of him.

"God made a mistake creating the two of you." Bruchner grinned wryly. "I must correct the mistake. Today one of you must die."

Bruchner looked at the boys who stood in front of him, naked and trembling with fear. Then, spreading a steady cloud of schnapps aroma, he went up to one of the twins, took a small coin from his pocket, and put it in the boy's hand.

"Toss the coin," Bruchner said casually. "If it falls heads up, you're lucky; if tails up – you are not. Isn't that fair?" He laughed, showing his yellow teeth.

But the boy threw the coin away. Bruchner glared at the boy, and then his face grew red. He drew his gun from its holster and touched it to the boy's temple, ready to pull the trigger.

"Are you tired of life, Jewish shit?" he asked, smiling.

Suddenly Bruchner changed his mind. Still keeping the gun on the boy's temple, Bruchner put his brother's hand on it.

"Kill him," he requested, "and you'll save your life." He left the gun in the boy's hand, and stepped aside.

The boy pulled the trigger. Bruchner grinned.

"Give him a chocolate bar," he told the Polish guard standing nearby.

Then he went to his office.

The next day Bruchner appointed Aaron Fisher a capo of the barracks, the informer finished his report.

Jacob covered his face with both hands. Only a witness to that horrible event could have written the detailed note about it; only a surviving witness. Why had he waited for almost forty years? Maybe he had recognized his former camp capo in the successful businessman Aaron Fisher? Maybe he was envious of the man's success after the war? Maybe this anonymous person simply wanted to remind the U.S. citizens, before he had died, that not everything could be forgiven? We would never know who that anonymous Holocaust survivor had been…

But how could Aaron Fisher carry such an inhuman burden on his soul for more than sixty years? Wasn't his dead twin brother much happier than he was?

Jacob felt a spasm in his throat. He pressed hand over his mouth to suppress it, but it didn't help. He burst out of crying as if the inhuman pain that Aaron Fisher had carried for more than sixty years was his own.

When Jacob at last recovered his senses, he knew why Aaron Fisher had visited Rabbi Lieberman so frequently. The rabbi was a *tzaddik*, and only the *tzaddik* could make Aaron Fisher's burden easier; to give him, if not forgiveness, but at least ease. Maybe he was close to committing suicide, and conversations with Rabbi Lieberman allowed him to regain hope for forgiveness from Above?

Jacob sat motionless for a long time. Switching the computer off, he knew definitely that he had to discard Aaron Fisher's name from his short list.

11.

Since Jacob had reestablished his relationship with his father after Rabbi Lieberman's death, he tried not to pass Shabbat dinners at his father's house. They gave him a long-forgotten feeling of the family hearth. He had also become much closer to his sister Tamar and her family. He had found her husband Barry to be a clever and wise man who wasn't obsessed with making money, as he thought about Barry before. Jacob found his two nieces to be wonderful and beautiful creatures. He had discovered that Bertha was not a dry, old woman, but rather a caring, lovely person. He had re-discovered his own family.

This Friday evening, as usual, Jacob went to his father's home. It was almost the time for lighting the candles. But to his surprise, besides the members of the family, two more people were sitting at the table to take part in the Shabbat prayer. When Jacob came in, Moses introduced him.

"This is my son Jacob, Leon. I think you had seen him last time when he was a teenager," Moses said, addressing to the man, and then added, "This is my old friend Dr. Leon Brodsky and his daughter Sarah."

"Time flies," Jacob said, bowing them.

"Time flies," Dr. Brodsky agreed. "I would never recognize you, Jacob."

Dr. Leon Brodsky was Moses' fellow-worker. They had maintained a friendship since the time when both had worked at Maimonides Hospital.

Dr. Brodsky was seventy-four years old, but he looked younger than Moses. His face seemed strange to Jacob until he realized what caused such an impression. Dr. Brodsky's eyebrows rose and fell like two pump handles. He was a bald man with a fringe of white hair around the bottom of his head. But his penetrating, clever Jewish eyes diminished all visible defects that you noticed at first glance. Your final impression was that you saw a clever Jewish doctor in front of you. And it was correct.

Dr. Brodsky shook Jacob's hand with a strong grip. "I'm glad to see you again, young man." Then he turned to a young lady sitting near him, "This is my daughter, Sarah."

"My pleasure," Jacob said, pressing slightly her hand.

Looking at Sarah, Jacob thought she, with her round, open face, couldn't be called a beautiful woman who attracted a man's attention at his first glance. But she had a steady charm.

"You are also a doctor as your father?" he asked her.

"No." Sarah smiled. "I work as an animation artist at Paramount Studios," she said.

"It's a great occupation for a woman," Jacob agreed.

The time of Shabbat had come. Both Jacob's nieces lit the candles, and then Moses read a short prayer:

"Baruch ata adonay, Adonay elocheiny, Adonay echad; Melech aolam, asher kidshany bemitzvotav vetsivany, leadlik ner shel Shabbat kodesh."

Everybody said, *"Amen,"* and then proceeded with Shabbat dinner.

As Jacob sat near Sarah, he asked her several questions for small talk. To his surprise, she turned out to be an interesting interlocutor, having her own, and not at all trivial, opinions on most subjects.

"I have always considered artists who create animated movies for children to be the happiest people in the world. Are you happy with your work, Sarah?" Joseph asked.

"I definitely am."

"Do you tally self-satisfaction in your creations?"

Sarah laughed. "Now I see that you are really a detective, Jacob, as your father told us at your absence," she said. "Art is an endless world," she added casually.

"I know one gifted painter who had never sold his pictures. When I asked him why, he told me that for him, it would be like selling a part of his soul," Jacob said.

Sarah looked at him attentively. "I understand that man," she said thoughtfully. "I would also never sell my pictures."

"So I was right when I had asked you whether you were satisfied with your work at the Studio."

"No, Jacob, I'm quite satisfied. My job is work for other people; my paintings are work for my soul."

"I'd like to look at them," Jacob said sincerely. "What are they? Water colors, portraits?"

"You'll be disappointed. They're religious paintings."

"Religious?" Jacob's surprise was sincere.

"Yes, they are all dedicated to the Messiah's coming," Sarah said carefully and looked at Jacob's face. "Are you surprised?"

"Not at all," Jacob objected. "I am intrigued and eager to look at them. May I?"

"Why not?" Sarah wrote down her telephone number. "Give me a call beforehand, okay?"

"I will, "Jacob promised firmly. "Do you live in Manhattan?" he asked as he saw the area code 212.

"I live in my father's house. But I rent a small studio with a co-worker who's also an artist," Sarah explained. "It's not in the exclusive area; it's a loft in an old building on the Twelfth Avenue, overlooking the Hudson River."

*

After all guests had gone, Moses and Jacob went to the library and sat in the armchairs placed near the electric fire. It didn't produce any heat, but did create a feeling of coziness.

"How did you like Sarah?" Moses asked carefully.

"Nice girl," Jacob said. "She's pretty and clever." He paused. "But I'm in no hurry to marry again, dad. I've had a negative experience in that field."

"That's right, negative," Moses agreed. "But you don't have a positive one to compare it to." He smiled. "I won't hurry you, but I would like for you to have a wider circle of acquaintances. Life is not restricted to only murder investigations."

"I know, dad," Jacob said warmly and pressed his father's hand slightly.

Then Jacob told his father about his search for people who could be involved in soul transfusion with the late Rabbi Lieberman.

"One of the people who had frequently visited Rabbi Lieberman and who attracted my attention is Ben Friedman by name. Is that name familiar to you, dad?"

"Ben Friedman?" Moses repeated. "He's a professor of philosophy at NYU. But he is not a *kabbalahist*. I'd call him a populist."

"A populist?"

"Yes. He delivers lectures about the secret path to God via soul travel. It has nothing in common with *Kabbalah*. His views are based on esoteric sciences – a great quantity of literature has been produced by followers of the Hindu and Vedanist religions."

"It's too foggy for me, dad. Why do you call this man a populist?"

"Eastern philosophy is popular with intellectuals, and Ben Friedman exploits its popularity. He tells people that man's chief delusion is his conviction that there are other causes at work in his life than his own state of consciousness. He considers that all that happens to man, comes to him because of his state of consciousness. This is why a change of consciousness is always necessary before one can begin to successfully travel in spiritual worlds, especially when alone. I want to emphasize this word, Jacob, *travel*. That wasn't the point of Rabbi Lieberman's teachings. I should say that Professor Friedman's point was that concentrated observation is a preparation toward the separation of the spirit from the body. It's strictly in accordance with Eastern philosophy; but it's far from the *Kabbalah*," Moses repeated. Then he glanced at Jacob. "I would recommend that you attend his lectures. You'll receive a fresh impression about his views, and also the man himself."

"I will, dad," Jacob agreed.

12.

Jacob's dog Charley was a good listener. He looked at Jacob with his clever eyes as if he understood every word he heard. But Charley kept silent. Silence is the highest level of understanding between friends. Sometimes Jacob thought he needed not only the silent approval of what he said, but also friendly objections because in many cases the truth was born in an argument. How could Charley object? Even if Jacob told Charley that he had to die, the dog would approve it silently because it was Jacob's decision.

Unexpectedly, Jacob had found a true friend who could not only listen to him, but also would express opinions that could contradict with his own.

If, several weeks ago, someone had told him that he would become a friend with a woman, Jacob would have smiled indulgently. Despite the fact that he had no pre-marital sexual experience, he believed that friendship between a man and a woman was possible in only one case – if they had passed through the sexual relations. His friendship with Sarah proved that he was wrong. Their friendship began after he had visited her studio.

*

A week after they had met each other at his father's house for Shabbat's dinner, Jacob gave Sarah a call.

"Hi, Sarah! Do you remember Sherlock Holmes whom you have recently met on Shabbat?

"Who can forget Sherlock Holmes? Are you still fighting with Professor Moriarti?" she asked, and Jacob understood that she not only had heard the famous detective's name, but also had read the novel written by Arthur Conan Doyle.

"I'm still eager to look at your paintings; you had promised me, Sarah," Jacob reminded her.

"I didn't forget, Jacob. I'll be glad to see you in my studio."

They fixed a day and time, and he hung up.

*

Two days later, at four o'clock, Jacob reached the red brick, seven story building. He found the building without difficulty. Industrial structures surrounded it, but four nearby skyscrapers had already changed the landscape of the area. Jacob thought that in several years, an ordinary man would not be able to buy an apartment in the area; real estate prices were skyrocketing.

Jacob took the elevator to the top, seventh floor, and rang the bell. A young blonde opened the door and looked at him questioningly. Jacob thought that he'd rung for the wrong apartment.

"Sorry," he said. "Obviously I am mistaken. I'm looking for Ms. Sarah Brodsky."

The blonde smiled. "You aren't mistaken, sir. I'm her roommate. We share this studio. Please, come in."

As Jacob came in, she said, "Sarah has just called. She stuck in heavy traffic on the Queensboro Bridge, and asked to be excused for her delay. She'll be here in half an hour. I must also be off; so I'll leave you alone. If you like paintings, enjoy, look around. You won't be able to mix up our pictures." She smiled. "By the way, my name is Marlene."

"I'm Jacob."

"I know your name. Sarah has described you perfectly." Marlene smiled, looking at Jacob openly.

In his forty-one, Jacob could be called a handsome man. His hair was still naturally dark, contrasting sharply with white temples. His eyes were covered by slightly tinted glasses. He wore the glasses since the time when a smiling Gipsy girl on the street had offered him to forecast his future. Jacob remembered her words that his eyes were like an opened book for everybody who wanted to know his fate.

When Marlene left, Jacob wandered through the loft, a former commercial warehouse. Only an artist could call it a dwelling, but it was perfect for an artist's studio. Bright afternoon sun lit every corner of the studio where he noticed about ten canvases. Only three of them were on easels; the rest leaned on one wall. Joseph easily separated Marlene's paintings from her roommate's. They were a woman's paintings – mostly Hudson River views – "*natura morte,*" dead nature. They didn't impress him too much.

Then Jacob saw a triptych that hypnotized him. He thought that these canvases could only have been painted by a Jew. The pictures were done in different styles, mostly post-impressionism. He saw the torso of a young Jew, coiled with heavy chains like a Laokon coiled with snakes. Although his face was not painted realistically, a viewer felt the inhuman pain in his eyes. Another composition made Jacob shrug – a woman holding the broken pieces of her heart in her palm. The third canvas of the triptych caused no less of a strong impression; naked bodies of Jewish slaves in front of the burning Temple stooped under the burden of chains.

Jacob was more than impressed by the pictures he saw. He thought it was not a woman's painting. Among all the paintings he had ever seen in museums that belonged to women's brushes, none were done in such a strong, philosophical, male manner.

Jacob was sitting in front of those canvases, having forgotten about time. At last he transferred his glance to the only canvas that was covered by a drape. He went to it and removed the linen.

He couldn't understand the feelings that flooded him. If the triptych impressed, this canvas shocked. It was still unfinished – only a combination of white colors in which one could see some kind of an image; but Jacob couldn't tell an image of what. Something illusive, unreal, and fantastic was captured on the canvas. Jacob couldn't cut his glance from the image, feeling as if he was looking into himself, into his soul.

The more Jacob looked at this canvas, the more the light coming from it attracted him. Like Mona Lisa attracted a spectator with the mystery of her smile, the picture in front of him attracted Jacob with an unknown mystery. He couldn't explain what the mystery was. The light had a magic force. Jacob felt that he wanted to dive into it, forget about his own 'I', and to become a part of this light. He felt an unrestricted wish to kneel before the canvas.

And he would have knelt if he hadn't heard Sarah's voice as she entered the room.

"Sorry, Jacob, that I'm late. The traffic was awful. Some idiot had jumped from the bridge. Are you tired of waiting for me?" she said, dashing in the loft.

Sarah crossed the floor to kiss him on the cheek like an old acquaintance. In the light of the setting sun that had filled the room, she glowed with an Eastern style of beauty. She had a certain plumpness of form that seemed to add rather than take away from her general beauty.

"Looking at your canvases, Sarah, I forgot about the time," Jacob said frankly. "I would call your paintings outstanding, but it wouldn't be the proper word. You are a genius, Sarah."

"Don't flatter me, Jacob."

"I don't."

"What paintings did you like?"

"Everything!" Jacob exclaimed emotionally. "You have to arrange an exhibition."

"I don't know. My painting is too personal." She shook her head and considered saying nothing more.

"Looking at your pictures, I had felt the pain in your soul. It's not personal, Sarah; it's the pain of the Jewish people." Jacob paused, and then looked at her. "What did you call that picture?" He pointed to the canvas that shocked him.

Not answering, Sarah went to a bookshelf, took down a book and opened it. Then she read:

"And the Lord spoke to Moses, saying: See I have called by name Bezaleel, the son of Uri, the son of Hur, of the tribe of Judah; and I have filled him with the Spirit of God, in wisdom, and in understanding, and in knowledge, and in all manner of

workmanship, to devise cunning works, to work in gold and in silver, and in brass, and in cutting of stones, to set them, and in carving of timber, to work in all kinds of workmanship. And I, behold I have given with him Aholiab, the son of Ahisamach, of the tribe of Dan; and in the hearts of all that are wise-hearted I have put wisdom that they make all that I have commanded thee: the tabernacle of the congregation, the arc of the testimony, and the mercy-seat that is thereupon, and all the furniture of the tabernacle."

The light deepened in Sarah's eyes, and a rare, rich cadence filled her voice as she read the Holy Words.

With a reverent touch, Sarah closed the book and replaced it on the shelf. She lifted her eyes to the light streaming down through the skylight.

As if burned by the light streaming from Sarah's eyes, Jacob kept silent. He couldn't guess clearly what she was talking about. He felt a harmony between Sarah's soul and her work, and he was afraid of breaking it with his question.

For a moment a look of a pain swept over Sarah's face. Then, as she became conscious of her hand's touch upon the easel, her eyes traveled to the exquisite work, and a light of a new hope swept the pain off her face.

"I don't know, Jacob, what happened to me when I read those words for the first time," she said frankly. "It seemed that my painting didn't depend on me at all. Like someone else moved my hand, I only held the brush," she whispered. "I felt I was God in happiness for myself, in strength and in light," Sarah said, feeling a vortex of feelings which pulled her deeper. But she couldn't express it in the plain English words.

Jacob's eyes lingered a moment on the rare and beautiful

picture, as Sarah said quietly, "I called this canvas 'Messiah's Coming.'"

Unexpectedly Jacob remembered the words that had remained in his mind since his youth," *And the Prince in the midst of them, when they go in, shall go in; and when they go forth, shall go forth.*"

He raised his eyes with deep, holy rapture shining in his entire face. His lips moved, but no sound came from them. His hand lay on Sarah's; it was a moment of a rare unity of their souls.

In the midst of their rapt devotion, the door of the studio opened. The slight sound aroused the dreamers, and they turned their faces in the direction of the door.

"Ah, Marlene!" Sarah exclaimed in greeting, and went to give her a hug.

The draft from the open door nipped gently at Sarah's dress, making her silhouette all the more breathtaking in Jacob's view. Marlene's eyes registered his glance at Sarah. She smiled understandingly.

"I thought you might be hungry, and picked up some Chinese food."

"That's fine," Sarah said, trying to seem casual.

"While waiting for Sarah, I enjoyed looking at your paintings, Marlene," Jacob said, trying to please her.

"Really?" She stared at him, still skeptical, but she was glad to hear the compliment. "My pictures aren't as gloomy as Sarah's. I told her many times that she needs to change themes, but she's stubborn." Marlene chuckled, and then added, "But she is very talented. I think one day her pictures will be in great demand."

"Dream and you'll be happy." Sarah smiled mildly. She let her gaze, but not her mind, drift.

"Why not? Everything depends on Above." Jacob agreed.

"Sarah believes that Messiah is coming," Marlene said, eating. "How about you, Jacob? Do you think the same?"

"Every Jew believes that, Marlene. Perhaps, when Passover comes again and we set His chair to enter, He will suddenly come. Let's wait." A dreamy smile broke out across Jacob's face. He stood up.

"Thank you, ladies, for a wonderful evening. And thank you for your wonderful art," Jacob said heartily. He kissed both on their cheeks. Reluctantly, he turned away and went down to his car.

Who knows, he thought again when he was sitting in the driver's seat. Maybe Sarah has seen what we still cannot see, and He is coming soon. Everything's maybe.

13.

Since Jacob experienced that unique feeling of his soul's unity with Sarah in her studio, they had become close friends. He called her often, not only to hear her opinion on one or another subject, but also simply to hear her soft voice.

Now he rarely talked to Charley. The dog who sat near him, quietly as usual, looked at Jacob with his clever, devoted canine eyes. If he could speak, he would ask Jacob whether Jacob still considered Charley his friend.

Sometimes, lying in bed, Jacob tried to analyze his feelings for Sarah.

If he needed her so much, if she had become a part of his life, was it the love that he had been waiting for all his life?

He liked Sarah; liked her clever eyes, her wit, her smile, her beautiful artistic hands, even her plumpness. But it wasn't love, and he knew it.

Jacob knew what had stopped transferring all of those feelings into love. It was her paintings; really it was one canvas, "Messiah's Coming."

Jacob realized that Sarah had become a harbinger of the Messiah's coming. She had received an artistic impulse strictly from Above; she had touched another, higher, spiritual world. It was a world where material things did not exist, as if Sarah herself already did not belong to the world of *Breishit* where Jacob and all other people lived. Since everything was forecast from Above, every meeting and every feeling, it would be stupidity to persuade himself that he was falling in love. He was not.

*

As soon as Jacob opened the door of the café where he had chosen to have a chat with Sarah, he smelled the welcoming aroma of fresh baking bread. He chose a table on the outside terrace. Sitting there, Jacob saw that the waitress bringing his drink was also guiding a guest to his table. Smiling with pleasure, he rose. Sarah settled in the chair he held out for and told the waitress to bring a glass of water. He had an ulterior motive for inviting Sarah to lunch, intending to tell her about Rabbi Lieberman and the investigation of the mystery of his death. He needed to share that mystery.

Jacob watched her every movement. He thought that Sarah had never looked more charming. He was ready to pay her a pretty compliment, saying that men around her were fools not to marry her. But at the last moment, Jacob bit his lips as he realized it could sound like a hint for her to their possible future love affair.

"Sarah, I love you like a sister, more than a sister," he said. "I have even told you everything about my personal life, as you are my closest friend." Jacob paused and drained his glass of water in two gulps.

He didn't see Sarah's color heightened visibly when she heard the word 'sister,' then her face became pale.

After Jacob emptied the glass, he continued, "Now I'm involved in the most important investigation of my life."

Sarah has already regained her composure, so gazed at Jacob with a question in her eyes. Jacob proceeded to tell her about Rabbi Lieberman's death, the letter "*alef*" he had seen on the rabbi's chest, and his deep feeling that there was someone whose actions had caused the rabbi's death.

While Jacob was talking, Sarah was a quiet companion, but she listened to every word with great interest. When Jacob finished his tale, she sat silently for several seconds, still under the influence of Jacob's words, intrigued. Then she took a deep breath. Shimmering eyes regarded Jacob thoughtfully.

"Even if your feeling is right, Jacob, you will never prove anything. What you talk about is the world of the spirit. What do we know about its laws? Obviously Rabbi Lieberman's death was punishment for an attempt at penetrating into another world. Are we, the people who live on the Earth, pure enough for that trip? We have to live in our world, following God's commandments but not violating them." A strange sense of drowsiness began to steal over her.

"Death has a place in the real world, not in the world of dreams," Jacob objected. With a shake of his head, he then changed the subject. "Forget about my stupid work. Sometimes it drives me crazy." He put his hand on hers. "I'm still under the deep influence of your painting."

Sarah returned his smile and turned her deep eyes toward him.

"Painting is a world of emotions. Understand emotions, and you can become a painter. I don't know why it's mostly an occupation for men," she said.

"Stating that painting is a world of emotions, Sarah, you

93

gave the answer to your own question. Men try to understand emotions; women don't. That's why it's a male occupation. Paintings cannot reflect the world of emotions on canvases; emotions are beyond it. Among all the pictures I've ever seen, only your 'Messiah's Coming' reflects the entire specter of human emotions; that's why it's unforgettable. If you've seen it once, you will never forget it because life itself is only symbolic of the soul."

Jacob's cell phone rang, startling him, and Captain O'Burke's face came into the light as he said, "hello." Jacob listened for a moment, grunted and hung up. Then he said, "I'm sorry, but I have to go to the office. It's an emergency. My colleague was shot."

"I understand," Sarah said.

Jacob waved to the waitress and paid the bill. Then he bent and kissed her on the cheek. "Bye now, darling. I think next time we'll have more time to talk."

After Jacob left, Sarah sat motionlessly for a long time. She knew she loved him. But she also knew that Jacob would never share her feelings. Maybe she was not a woman who could bring happiness to a man? What a painful word – friendship! Why did God send her the meeting with Jacob? Did He want to make her suffer? What for? Didn't she deserve the same simple happiness that other women had – mutual love, family, and children?

Sarah shook her head to discard her gloomy thoughts. She had her work and her painting. She was a happy woman.

She drank her coffee, put her sunglasses on, and headed for the door.

14.

Professor of philosophy Benjamin Friedman was tall, bald, with a prominent, bobbing Adam's apple, a white-bearded man of that indifferent age when you could equally give him the age of sixty-nine or seventy-nine years. He had already completed his distinguished career as Dean of the NYU Faculty, but remained a visiting professor who, from time to time, delivered outstanding lectures on Eastern philosophy and soul traveling.

Jacob signed up to attend one of his lectures, *Unique Case Histories of Soul Travelers.* When he came to the overcrowded auditorium, he could hardly find an empty seat in one of the last rows. At eleven o'clock sharp, Professor Friedman approached the podium. He didn't carry a briefcase and had no papers or conspectus in his hands. From a distance he looked much younger, maybe because, unlike most of men of his age, he did not wear a wig or dye his hair. To Jacob, he seemed so natural and good-looking, that he forgot that Professor Friedman was one of the main suspects on his short list.

"Ending the last lecture," Professor Friedman began, "I

promised to lecture about unique case histories of soul travel. Recollecting such cases was in my attic." He knocked his head by his finger. "I decided to dedicate them a separate lecture which I offer to your attention."

As the use of tape recorders in Professor Friedman's lectures was prohibited, Jacob paid close attention to the fact that most of listeners were making conspectus of his words.

After a pause, Professor Friedman continued, "There are so many unique case histories of saints, spiritual heroes, holy men, and mystics who have done soul travel that they could fill several volumes. Regardless of whether or not one believes in out-of-body projection, sooner or later, as one travels the path to God, this experience will enter his life.

I have mentioned in my previous lectures that three schools of metaphysical thought sharply divided the thinkers in this field. First is the mental theory, held by those who believe in intellectualism; second, cosmic consciousness; and third, the soul-travel theory. Each school firmly believes in the path that they have chosen to reach Ultimate Reality.

Saint Paul is known to have been a student and practitioner of the cosmic-consciousness system. Yet he, by his own admission, recognized out-of-the-body travel in his writings. In II Corinthians, Paul said, 'I knew a man in Christ about fourteen years ago, (whether in the body I cannot tell, or whether out of the body I cannot tell; God knoweth); such a one caught up to the third heaven, into paradise, and heard unspeakable words, which are not lawful for a man to utter.'

Saint Paul clearly states that this man has a glorious experience in an out-of-body projection. This is the ultimate goal, to be reached while still occupying a physical body. He goes on to say that he envies such a man for his opportunity to be in paradise with God. Since God is far above the third heaven, Saint Paul made the mistake of thinking that it was the reality of all universes."

"Neither metaphysical theory nor cosmic conscience theory could have something in common with Rabbi Lieberman's views," Jacob thought. "Maybe the soul-travel theory can give the answer."

"We have cases like this daily," Professor Friedman continued. "Many people do not know what's happening to them and need to have some sort of yardstick in order to judge their own experience. Generally, the best yardstick in the beginning is to read about how others are able to do soul traveling, and what happens to them while outside their bodies.

Dozens of cases are on record of those who, while locked in prison, succeeded in out-of-body projection. One of such case came out as a piece of fiction written by George DuMaurier, the British novelist. The main protagonist of his novel, locked in prison for a life sentence for a crime that he did not commit, continued to visit his sweetheart in his ethereal body every night.

One of the classic cases of all times was that of Ed Morell, who was confined for four years in the Arizona state prison. His experiences were vouched by Jack London, who published Morell's story under the title *The Star Rover.*

The jailers subjected Morell to a level of torture comparable to those of the Spanish Inquisition. Morell would be laced tightly in a straight-jacket and left there for hours, once up to five days. Each time he would leave his physical body and roam the world outside, including the region of the stars. He would fall into a trance state caused by the torture and had himself soaring freely outside the prison walls.

Much of what Morell saw outside was checked and found to be true, though he himself was confined in an underground cell with no windows, and no one with whom to talk but his brutal jailers. After his release, Morell found, to his surprise, that he was unable to project except under the conditions of extreme agony.

One of the greatest cases in religious history is that of Shankar who, during the ninth century, left his body hidden in a tree trunk and spent time as the husband of a woman so that he might win a famous series of religion arguments with Mandana Misha and his equally learned wife Unhaya Bharati.

When he vanquished Mandana Misha, the wife challenged him to a debate on sex, a subject about which she had expert knowledge, and the young celibate had none at all. But he asked for month's postponement. In the interval, he was able to use his great yogi powers. He hid his body away in a tree trunk in a deep forest, entered the physical body of the dying king Amaruka, and mastered the mysteries of sex. When the month expired, Shankar returned, carried on the debate, and won over the famous woman scholar."

Jacob listened to Professor Friedman with interest, but couldn't discard a thought that everything he heard was some kind of a hallucination experience, nothing more. However Professor Friedman's erudition of the subject was extraordinary. Jacob was back to the lecture's subject.

"Among the early leaders in this field, we'll find the names of the ninth century Persian mystic Shams-i-Tabris, Moulana Rumi of Persia. Later we find Kabir, the sixteenth century Hindu mystic, Tulsi Dass, Guru Nanak, and their followers," Professor Friedman continued, impressing the audience with his memory. "Shams-i-Tabris was adept at getting in and out of his body. He was constantly subjected to attacks by bigots for his religious beliefs. Once when he was traveling between two major Persian cities, he was able to leave his body and look up the road to discover several men with clubs, who hid themselves behind a clump of brush, ready to kill him. As a result, he took another route and completely escaped the trap.

Here it's worth also mentioning a book written by Guru Paramahansa Yogananda. In his famous *Autobiography of a Yoga* he described the 360 degree vision he experienced. Later in his book, he speaks of his old guru Sri Yukesteswar returning to his other body from beyond the veils of death, and greeting him. The very touch of his old guru was like that of human flesh, while they embraced in the joy of the meeting again."

Professor Friedman paused only for a sip of water. The deep silence in the large auditorium reflected the highest level of the audience's interest. Jacob thought the professor was a unique man to be able to keep all those Indian and Persian names in his memory and to deliver his lecture without notes.

"You can think, my listeners, that only Eastern people experienced soul traveling," Professor Friedman continued after a pause. "But that's not so. Without a doubt, Emanuel Swedenborg, born in Stockholm in 1688, was one of the most remarkable projectionists in all religious history. He could visit the so-called dead, make trips into hell, and into heaven at his own volition, and at the same time, he made himself remarkably useful to his generation and to his country.

He left over twenty-five lengthy manuscripts about his trips into the other worlds, how he rescued victims from the pit of hell and carried them into heaven via some type of elevator lift. He said that he was saving them from time spent in purgatory by an act of kindness on God's part, who supposedly had appointed Swedenborg as a spiritual traveler in such matters.

One of his outstanding feats of soul travel was when visiting a friend in Gothenburg, some three hundred miles from Stockholm. During the dinner party, in the presence of more than fifteen people, he reported that a dangerous fire had broken out in South Stockholm, and was spreading rapidly. Later in the evening, he reported that it had been extinguished.

Napoleon is another famous man in history, who was able to leave his body. Tolstoy says in his novel *War and Peace* how Napoleon sat behind knoll playing cards with his officers while the battle of Austerlitz took place on December 5, 1805, against the Russians. He kept watch over the battle by direct projection. When he needed to send messages about troop movements to his commanders in the field, he was often ahead of those who sent couriers asking for permission for the same movements. At the same time, the Russian General Kutuzov was fighting the battle from his position in a tent, with similar tactics.

Alexander the Great could contribute his success of being established as a military genius to his ability to get out of his body and view what was taking place during the struggle between his army and the enemy. It is said that he stood outside his body while winning his three major battles, Gaugamela, Issus and Hydaspes, and was able to direct his troops efficiently because of his overall view of the battle."

When Professor Friedman took another short break, Jacob couldn't stop himself from asking him a question.

"In all the interesting cases you have mentioned, professor, how long can a soul travel outside the body? The body is supposed to die if the soul leaves it," Jacob remarked.

"That's a good question, young man." Professor Friedman looked at Jacob from beneath his glasses. "Neither Napoleon nor Alexander, for example, succeeded in the end for they used soul projection for a purpose unworthy of spiritual necessity. As a result, they had lost everything. But what does *time* mean? The Torah says the world was created in six days, *Kabbalah* says that every day lasts a thousand years. What does *time* mean?" Professor Friedman repeated thoughtfully. "From this position, we are talking about a jiffy."

Jacob would prefer to hear a more expansive answer to his question, but Professor Friedman continued the lecture.

"Apollonius of Tyana, the great Greek mystic of the second century B.C. was one who could easily be in two places at the same time and report back to the physical senses what was taking place at a distance. This great master could come and go as he wished. The Emperor Domitian saw Apollonius disappear from before the throne after the Emperor sentenced him to death. Apollonius was weighted with chains and surrounded by palace guards. He was there one moment, and the next, had disappeared, leaving nothing but the chains. Later it was recorded that within moments after disappearing from Domitian's sight, the famed adept appeared beside one of his chief disciples on a road some hundred miles away."

Professor Friedman continued talking about the most famous cases of soul travel. He mentioned Zarathustra of Zoroaster who lived in the eighth century B.C. and was the founder of the ancient Persian religion of Magi that later developed into what is known today as the Parsee faith; the mystery school of Pythagoras, the great adept of the fifth century B.C., Mohammed's journey into the heavenly world in the seventh century; Godic, a Saxon monk who lived in the twelfth century; Andrew Jackson Davis and Madam Blavatsky who lived in the nineteenth century.

But Jacob already listened to the lecture absent-mindedly. The subject was interesting, but far from the point of Jacob's interest.

At last Professor Friedman finished the demonstration of his outstanding knowledge of the subject with the words, "There are thousands of records in the library today, reporting out-of-the body experiences. It is a universal experience, but to all who experience or read about it, it seems to be unique. And only God knows what He can do. The true purpose of soul travel is to find God's heavenly realm; the realm where God has established His fountainhead in the center of all universes."

The lecture was inquisitive for Jacob, nothing more. He went up to the podium, and when Professor Friedman remained alone, asked him, "Why, among all the cases of soul travelers that you mentioned, professor, were there no Jewish mystics? The *Kabbalah* says there is a way to join a soul of *tzaddik*, doesn't it?"

Professor Friedman took his glasses off and looked at Jacob attentively. Then he sighed deeply.

"I think the world of the *Kabbalah* is not a mystical one, young man," he said. "The man, who can penetrate through the decoded Torah, can do everything. But who can penetrate through it? Obviously we can name some of great Jewish travelers: Rashi, Rashbi, Maimonidis… But that's not about soul traveling; it's much deeper. Only a rabbi can penetrate through it. Unfortunately I am not a rabbi." Then he added thoughtfully, "Maybe every Jew is a soul traveler; every time when we put the *tefillin* on..." Now Professor Friedman looked no younger that his seventy-nine years.

Jacob thanked Professor Friedman and left the auditorium. The first lecture hadn't given Jacob the answer to the questions as to whether the professor could be involved with the attempt of soul transfusion with Rabbi Lieberman. Too many questions remained without answers. Why did Professor Friedman carefully avoid questions about *Kabbalah* experiences in this field? Why, when talking about soul traveling, did he avoid mentioning soul connections? Why didn't he mention as a famous case of soul travelling the creation of *Zohar*? Maybe the next lecture, Jacob thought, would give him the answers. It would be delivered in a week. He had read the title of the next lecture - *Preparation for a Journey to God*. This time Professor Friedman must show his cards; otherwise, he wouldn't give the lecture such a title.

Let's wait for a week, Jacob decided finally.

15.

A week later Jacob was sitting in the same auditorium. This time he arrived earlier to find a seat in the first row; he wanted to study Professor Friedman's body language.

As always without a briefcase and any conspectus in his hands, the professor glanced over the overcrowded auditorium.

"I see most of the same faces. It means you haven't lost interest in my lectures. The title of the current one is *Preparation for the Journey to God.*"

He smiled. "Although none of us are in a hurry to take this journey, considering it to be the last one."

Professor Friedman saw Jacob sitting in the first row. In differ from other listeners, Jacob hadn't a notebook in his hands, and the professor paid attention to it.

"Traditional philosophy has left us powerless to free the individual and bring him to the independence he has longed for. It has left him swallowed up by its promises, and it has brainwashed him into thinking that he is only a puny part of God's great universe," the professor said as he addressed to Jacob personally. And then he began his lecture:

"The present systems of metaphysics are no longer of any use, for they only offer us, under the guise of the infinite, the consolation of death of the physical body. What they are telling us about the afterlife doesn't make sense when we come to know them through the spirit.

Every man faces the choice of having freedom via his individualistic self or becoming a part of the crowd that believes in materialistic miracles. It's the choice of living in an illusionary world or living vitally through the spirit. The true spiritual life consists of living to the fullest and developing the ability to leave the body at will in order to travel through the other worlds. Life is an infinite succession of 'nows.' It cannot be anything else.

The old classical expression is '*The truth is one; man calls it by various names.*' That only means that we shall set ourselves apart from life exterior, and live within the interior.

The main step in this direction, in preparation for the spiritual worlds, is that of being released from desire itself. The great paradox here is that when one wants nothing, he gets everything. This comes from getting rid of desire, as Buddha taught when he said that desire is the source of all pain. The end of all desires is the beginning of immortality.

We are aware that God Himself is not within us, but the kingdom of heaven is, and this kingdom of heaven is only that which we can call the spirit. We realize that we are available to God at all times because of this principle. This means that each plane of life is within us, and without the consciousness of man. Spirit, therefore, is the spark of God that is instilled in the consciousness of each individual, so that its consciousness – or soul – can be an operative force on its own, anywhere within the universe of the Supreme God."

Listening to Professor Friedman's lecture, Jacob began to

realize that Professor Lieberman's theory didn't bringing him any closer to the solution of the soul transfusion's enigma. The professor spoke of self-purification, and it, naturally, had led him to the point of self-hypnosis.

"If we start out by putting ourselves to sleep, the law of reversed effort starts working. The harder we try, the less we are able to do it. When a hypnotist wants to put us under control, he uses the law of reversed effort by getting his subject to overdo efforts to defeat the hypnotist. For example, there is the old hand-clasping test where the hands of the subject are locked together, and he is told by the hypnotist that 'you can't pull your hands apart; the harder you try, the more firmly they will stick together, and you will fail to resist my commands," Professor Friedman said, looking at Jacob. Usually he chose in the audience one person to whom he addressed delivering his lecture. Today this person was Jacob.

"This is exactly how man fails in movement of the soul. He is working with the mind in trying to get out of the body and the mind, which is influenced by one or all perversions, will keep informing him that he cannot get out of his body. The harder he tries, the more firmly will soul and body stick together, and he will fail in trying to resist the commands of his mind."

Professor Friedman paused, and Jacob again thought that everything the professor was talking about was no more than scientific justification of cases similar to those that he, Jacob, had witnessed in Amsterdam where Josephine had seen the face of her husband's killer.

"If you have any questions, please feel free to ask them," Professor Friedman said, again recognizing Jacob in the audience.

He made a short pause. As the listeners didn't ask questions, the professor was back to the lecture.

"If the state of free thinking, freedom and viewpoint is to be obtained, some method for getting out of the body and making contact with spiritual travelers must be established."

At having heard those last words, Jacob was all ears as Professor Friedman continued, "The concepts brought about by certain thinkers cannot be true for anyone who has had God-realization. The God-realized dwell in positive worlds, in the spiritual levels, and do not swing back and forth like those living in the body. He is in this world, but not of it."

The hint that the lecture was at the point of interest for Jacob again became a phantom.

"The old Chinese concept of Yang and Yin is a good example of this swinging back and forth between the two poles. Yang and Yin are positive and negative principles, male and female, the light and dark of life. It's the law of polarity, what we might call the law of opposites. This means that nothing can exist without its opposite. Without the mountains, there can be no valleys. Without shadows, there can be no perception of light. There can be no such thing as evil unless we can compare it with good. Without wisdom, there can be no ignorance and without age, no youth.

The concept of Yang and Yin goes back to the misty time of history's beginning. Yang is always considered the abstract, and Yin, the concrete, or we might say the spiritual and the material. Yang and Yin play an important part in the preparation of ourselves for soul travel, Cause and Effect are the basic principles of the lower worlds, and this we see in the eminent *Kabbalah* which states 'as above, so below.' This is one of the first principles of metaphysical works. The outer or material world is a reflection of the inner or higher world, the macrocosmic world. Everything that exists in outer, or material world, also has existence in the higher, or astral world –the first world of the within."

Professor Friedman again mentioned *Kabbalah*, and again Jacob realized that all the professors' words were only general statements about self-consciousness and possibility that everyone should not restrict themselves by the tight frames of material world. He definitely did a good job, showing one of the ways to find the truth. Was it interesting to Jacob? It definitely was. Was it useful for his investigation? Obviously not.

Jacob continued listening to the lecture absent-mindedly.

"God is a spirit and must be worshipped in spirit and truth. This means that the Ultimate Being is a spirit, or rather a spirit that is part of itself, and we can only know Him through and by this part of the whole. So man must learn to give up the flesh, and allow for the perfection of the soul to take over. Man must learn to be guided into that highest state of consciousness that we call the God-consciousness. No teacher can force us to realize the higher planes of the elevated states of consciousness. This must be done by ourselves alone. This is why spiritual travelers stand by at all times to watch our progress, not raising a hand unless we call upon them for assistance."

Professor Friedman had finished the lecture. He looked at Jacob as if he was the only man to whom his lecture was delivered. But Jacob asked no questions.

Now he definitely knew that Professor Friedman could not be a partner in Rabbi Lieberman's experiment. But why did he visit Rabbi Lieberman so often? Obviously as a scientist, he didn't feel any satisfaction about what he had studied; he couldn't surmount the restricted bounders of the subject. He felt there was a much deeper field concealed in the *Kabbalah* that he couldn't explain it. Maybe he felt, at the end of his life, that he was going in the wrong direction?

Only one name remained on Jacob's short list…

16.

The month of Jacob's vacation had passed much too quickly. The only progress from his investigation was that he had clarified the person that he suspected to be Rabbi Lieberman's partner in the experiment that caused his death.

As soon as Jacob returned to his office, he reported to Captain O'Burke. At seeing Jacob, O'Burke smiled.

"Jack, we missed you! How did you spend your vacation?"

Jacob made an indifferent gesture. "Did some homework that needed to be done," he said casually.

"There's nothing to be done. Our homework is also necessary," O'Burke agreed. Then he added, "I'll give you one file to work on. It needs to be closed as soon as possible. The daughter-in-law of our consul to St. Petersburg, Russia, was found dead. She drowned in the river; not in the Neva River in St. Petersburg, but here, in the Hudson River. In addition to everything else, she's Russian, a naturalized citizen. You'll work with the FBI, and maybe the CIA. Isn't that a nice way to start after a vacation?" O'Burke grinned, handing Jacob the folder.

"Yes, that's nice," Jacob agreed with a grumble.

Going to his office, submerged in thoughts that this 'nice' work would take all his time, Jacob bumped into a man. He began to apologize when he heard, "Jack, I'm glad to see you, old chap!"

Jacob glanced at the man and recognized Harold Fiedler, the lawyer for the "Princess of Harlem," who had persuaded him not to press charges against her.

"Hi, Harold," Jacob said indifferently. "Are you still lobbying for another 'princess'?"

"No," Harold said. "She's dead. Haven't you read the papers?"

"Dead?" Jacob raised his brow in sincere surprise.

"Yes, the stupid girl caused another collision. She was drunk again. This time it cost her life. Stupidity is always punishable," Harold said with a casual wave of his hand.

"She would be alive if you and your liberal friends had put her in jail," Jacob remarked.

Harold smiled and changed the topic.

"Two days ago I thought of you, Jack," he said.

"Really?" Jacob asked mockingly. "In what connection?"

"I'm going to start my own business, and I need a partner," Harold said carefully.

When Jacob kept silent, he explained. "You're a lawyer, Jack. How do you like the name 'Fiedler and Reterseil, Attorneys at Law' for the company? It sounds good to me."

Jacob laughed. "To be a trial lawyer, a man must have a different mentality from mine. I wouldn't struggle to set a murderer free, knowing he was a murderer. You have to be a Robert Shapiro to receive moral satisfaction at the acquittal of a double murderer as he did in the O.J. Simpson's case. And I don't think money is the equivalent of moral satisfaction.

Thanks for the offer, but find another partner, Harold." Jacob touched Harold's shoulder, and went on along the corridor.

I told Sarah that after the Rabbi Lieberman's case I was going to change my profession, he thought. That was irresponsible. Everything that I can do with is being a police investigator.

In the office Jacob sat at the desk and opened the file that O'Burke had given him. The investigation had already collected several documents, formal information. The dead woman, Ana Turnikov, was the daughter-in-law of Norman Winder, an American consul in St. Petersburg, Russia. She was a naturalized U.S. citizen, a dentist who graduated from NYU Dental School. She and her husband had two children, four and eight years old. Ana's husband was Norman Winder's son from his first marriage. Unlike many other divorcees, Norman Winder kept a friendly relationship with his first wife who lived in California. He had also had a son of sixteen from his second marriage. There were nothing suspicious; no complaints of domestic violence; a happy family.

When Ana's body was found in the Hudson River, Norman Winder was in St. Petersburg. There were no tracks of sexual abuse or robbery; neither her expensive Cartier watch nor two-carat diamond ring was taken from her hand. Was it suicide? That was hardly to be expected, Jacob thought. She had never visited a psychiatrist. It's not an easy case, Jacob thought. It'll take much time. He closed the folder.

Despite the fact that Jacob normally would have been interested in working on such a case, now all his thoughts were occupied with Rabbi Lieberman's death enigma. He couldn't stop in the middle of the road. If he began with Rabbi Lieberman's death investigation, he had to finish it. Unfortunately, the new work would take a lot of time that he would have dedicated to Rabbi Lieberman's case. Now the new case was only a routine job for him. But it had to be done also, even though it would take much time. There was nothing to be done. He was a police officer, he didn't belong to himself.

As always in rare cases of professional powerlessness, Jacob felt baseless irritation. Then he calmed himself as he decided to talk to his father.

He put the new file in the safe and left his office.

"I'm leaving," he told Captain O'Burke on the way out. Then he explained, "I need a breath of fresh air. I don't have any ideas."

"Breathe deeply." O'Burke grinned. "I need this case finished as quickly as possible."

Jacob made an indifferent gesture in answer.

17.

So Jacob didn't wait until Shabbat to go to his father's house. At seeing him in the door, Bertha was not surprised.

"Jacob," she said, following him to the hall. "I've got an idea; why don't you move in here? We have two empty rooms, and you'll save all the money for your Manhattan apartment rent." She grinned.

"That's not a bad idea," Jacob said, embracing her. "I'll think it over. The main reason I didn't do it before, I care for you, Bertha. If I move in, it will be twice the work for you. And I've become accustomed to my bachelor life. It has a lot of advantages."

"And a lot of disadvantages," said Moses who appeared in the hall door. "But I'm afraid I'm too old for a fruitful discussion on that topic."

"Are you hungry, Jacob?" Bertha asked.

"No. Thank you, Bertha. I've already had lunch."

Moses and Jacob went to the library and placed themselves in their chairs.

"You don't look fresh, son," Moses said.

"I'm not," Jacob agreed. "I hope to rest after we've solved Rabbi Lieberman's death mystery."

"Are you heading in the right direction, son?"

"I'm going nowhere, dad. I've stopped because I have no clue about how to approach the man who did it. Only you can help me because only you can approach him."

"Me?"

"As a scientist and as the author of cabalistic treatises, you have much in common to discuss with him. Nothing creates closer contacts than a professional discussion."

"Maybe you're right, son," Moses said thoughtfully. "He has published a wonderful book recently, and I'd like to express my opinions about it. I can use that publishing as a reason to correspond with him."

With these words, Moses handed Jacob a book. He opened it and read the title, *Zohar.*

"Another *Zohar*?" Jacob gave Moses a surprised look.

Moses smiled. "It's not *Zohar*; it's about *Zohar*. It's a book of commentaries on *Zohar*, written by Rabbi Aharon Korinetz. It's written in English, not in Hebrew, so it will be perfectly understandable for you. Some commentaries are controversial, and it may be a point of discussion. The discussion is a fruitful way, a starting point of a professional relationship."

"It's a plausible reason to contact the author," Jacob agreed. "But such a discussion is 'two to tango.' How can I approach this man?"

Moses looked at his son, and irony sparkled in his eyes.

"I'll tell him you're a writer, who is going to write a book about the history of the Lubavich movement, for instance. It sounds plausible, doesn't it? And by the way, why can't you try to write such a book, Jacob?"

"To become a writer, a man must be born a writer; it's from God." Jacob smiled.

"It's from God," Moses agreed. "But no writer began writing until he had gained enough life experience. Your experience as a police detective much exceeds the experience of an ordinary man."

"I would agree with you, dad, if we were talking about fiction literature. But a history of the Lubavich movement would be a documentary; a specific documentary. It can be written by only an insider."

"Bingo! Jews living among gentiles, naturally begin copying their life style. The results are comic or pathetic. They stop being Jews. I think sometimes why we, Chasidic Jews, wear the clothes of the eighteenth century. We look funny to gentiles, but our clothes differs us from them. Was it worth changing clothes? Can you imagine *tzitzit* above the modern suit? It would be more than funny; it would be comic. But *tzitzit* are in harmony with the suit of the eighteenth century. Many Jews wear a *kipa*, but it doesn't make them more Jewish if they don't wear *tzitzit*, do not put *tefillin,* and violate many other requirements of the Torah. For the same reason, Arabs wear the clothes that they wore four or five centuries ago: living in Rome, do not do what the Romans do if you want to remain that you are."

Although Moses was talking about 'other Jews,' Jacob thought that his father was talking about him.

"In this case Jews must discard all the other attributes of civilization, such as cell phones, cars, TV… Is that possible?" Jacob asked.

"No. But we have to try to limit their influence on our life."

"That is impossible, dad!"

"Alas! That's the problem with our identity and fulfill-ment of God's commandments."

"Unfortunately, the Jews violate God's commandments even on the Land of Israel. We are not beyond society."

Moses sighed. "Israel is a state for Jews, but she is not a Jewish state. Today's Israel is a secular state, and it is histori-cal nonsense. She was created by left-wing socialists-commu-nists who were far from God. Realistically, today we have two states: one is a secular state ruled by self-hating Jews who are far from God, and the second is the religious Israel where religion is worshipped for the sake of religion. Leaders of both states think only about satisfaction of their ambitions. And the most awful thing is that both Israeli states contra-dict God's will. Can we forecast the collapse of Israel in the nearest future? Or does it not matter at all in the light of the fact that the Messiah is soon coming? I don't know," Moses said thoughtfully. "It's too painful to talk about." Then he abruptly changed the topic. "But life consists of more than resolving the problems that we create ourselves; God gave us too much to enjoy. Have you seen Sarah since the day you had met her in my home?"

"I have, dad. And I'm really grateful to you for our acquaintance; Sarah is one of the most interesting women I've ever met. We're friends."

"Friends?" Moses could not hide his surprise.

"Close friends," Jacob clarified.

"And you have never seen her in any other aspect? She would be a good wife; she's clever and beautiful. What more does a man need?"

"The man who marries her will be a happy man," Jacob agreed. "But everything is from Above, dad, "Jacob said.

Then he told his father about the feelings he had

experienced in Sarah's art studio. Moses didn't interrupt Jacob's emotional speech. He understood him; Jacob was his son, his flesh, his soul.

"But I'd like to see you happy, son," Moses said softly and put his hand over Jacob's. Maybe friendship would be a step in the right direction, Moses thought. My boy deserves to be happy. I do hope Lord will hear my prayers.

As always when he was in the father's house, time flew. While saying good-bye and kissing Bertha's cheek, Jacob winked her.

"I'll think about your offer, Bertha."

"What offer?" asked Moses.

"It's a secret, dad." Jacob smiled cunningly, and went out.

Sitting in the car, he remembered his father's idea of writing a book about the Chassidic movement. Maybe God wants me to totally change my life after I would resign from my office? Only God knows, Jacob thought and switched the ignition on.

18.

Moses was not too far from his decision to start his correspondence with Rabbi Aharon Korinetz. Using the case that he had recently read the rabbi's new book, Moses sent him a letter.

Dear Rabbi Korinetz:

With admiration and great pleasure, I have read your new book published under the title ZOHAR.

Written in plain English, it makes the most complicated pieces of the Torah clear for men's understanding and extends the limit of our understanding of the God's treasure.

Your message is eye opening. I think many readers will come to a deeper knowledge of the Kabbalah through your fascinating and convincing book.

> *Very truly yours,*
> *Dr. Moses Reterseil,*
> *New York, Boro Park.*

Taking into account the distance between Melbourne and New York, the answer was prompt; Moses received the response from the rabbi ten days later.

Dear Dr. Reterseil:

Thank you for the most positive evaluation of my modest work. My goal in writing Zohar was to attract the attention of a wide circle of Jewish readers to our eternal values, especially people who have not experienced a deep knowledge of Hebrew. This way leads, of course, to simplification, but also opens the gate to the abyss of knowledge.

As a cure, Hasidic philosophy holds the belief that God permeates all physical objects in nature, including all living beings. According to the sixth Lubavicher Rebbe Yosef Yitzchok Schneerson, God is all, and all is God.

In opposition, many Jewish religious rationalists misunderstand, believing that this seemingly pantheistic doctrine is a violation of the Mimodean principle of faith that God is not physical, and thus consider it heretical. In fact, Hasidic philosophy, especially the Chabad School, views all physical and psychological phenomena as relative and illusionary; God, the absolute reality in itself, is beyond all physical or even spiritual concepts and boundaries.

I tried to construct my book strictly in the boundaries of Hasidic philosophy, which teaches a method of contemplating God, as well as the inner significance of the Mitzvos (commandments and rituals of Torah law.)

I do hope my book will help to revive Jews both physically and spiritually, as it demands cultivating an extra degree of piety. From my point of view, my Zohar teaches that one should not merely strive to improve one's character by learning new habits and manners; but rather a person should completely change the quality, depth, and maturity of one's nature.

I believe also that the esoteric teachings of the Kabbalah can be made understandable to everyone. This understanding is meant to help refine a person, as well as adding depth and vigor to one's ritual observance.

If I managed to contribute to reaching one of the Hasidic goals, it would be a royal reward for me as an author.

> *Very truly yours,*
> *Rabbi Aharon Korinetz,*
> *Melbourne, Australia.*

After Moses had read Rabbi Korinetz' letter a second time, he thought that it wouldn't be easy to introduce Jacob to him as a writer. Will it be a plausible explanation that an inexperienced in theology author would like to write the history of the Hassidic Movement?

19.

The new task that Jacob had received from Captain O'Burke had shaded the mystery of Rabbi Lieberman's death for some time. He carefully studied all the information that he could pick up from the Ana Turnikov file. This case was also a mystery, and every mystery attracted Jacob like a prayer attracted a neophyte.

She was definitely murdered, he thought. He had reached that final conclusion. But why? And by whom? He had to find the answer, but he had no clue.

A talk with the Ana's husband, Jerry Winder, didn't clear up the situation. Both young people had studied together, loved each other, and after the marriage even worked together at the same hospital. Jacob decided to talk to Ana's father-in-law, Norman Winder, the U.S. vice-consul to St. Petersburg, Russia. Jacob had always relied on his ability to collect concealed information in personal contacts with people. So he again filled a travel form and went to Captain O'Burke's office.

"Captain, I need your permission to fly to Russia. I'd like to talk to Consul Winder."

"I'm beginning to realize, Jack, why you rarely take vacations; you prefer to rest at NYPD's expense." O'Burke grinned.

"You're clairvoyant, captain. You don't pay me enough to spend any money from my pocket, and, unfortunately, no one offers me bribes." Jack smiled. He liked this gymnastic play of words.

"I've caught that hint about raising your salary, Jack! Read my lips…"

Jacob laughed. "I know you'll do it as soon as the mayor stops budget cuts. But in this particular case, I won't insist on a first class ticket; I'll fly by coach."

"Taking into account such an essential saving, Jack, I won't object," O'Burke agreed, and signed the form.

When Jacob returned to his office, he booked a ticket and called Sarah.

"What about having lunch with me, Sarah? I'm preparing to fly to Russia, to St. Petersburg."

"To Russia? They say it's a very interesting country. I planed to spend my next vacation there. By the way, my ancestors were born there."

"In St. Petersburg?"

"No. As I know, they lived in Ukraine."

"That's not the same?"

Sarah laughed. "When the Soviet Union existed, it was the same; now they're different countries with one common feature – anti-Semitism."

"So I'll see you tomorrow to collect more information about Russia."

"Just for you, I'll try to refresh my memory, Jacob."

*

The next day Jacob was sitting at a café that he had remembered passing last night on his way home. It had a peculiar sign in front – it was a dancing duck. Why a dancing duck, he wondered, but remembered the place. Obviously it was a popular place; the café was clearly crowded. It took some time before he was lucky enough to occupy a table. When he saw Sarah entering the room, he waved her to the table. She wore big sunglasses with tinted lenses, which made her face mysterious. The glasses were not dark enough to totally hide her eyes; you saw them but couldn't read its expression. She was dressed in a well-tailored brown knit suit; her short hair reminded Jacob of his mother's style. He thought Sarah looked too conservative, but perfect for a Jewish companion.

"You look great," Jacob said frankly.

Sarah didn't answer the compliment, although felt his words were sincere.

"You look tired, Jacob," she said, giving him a hug. Then she sat down at the table. "I don't like it."

"I'm tired," Jacob agreed. "I'm doing two works simultaneously, and it disturbs me from concentration on Rabbi Lieberman's death." Then he changed the point. "What shall we eat? This place has a good reputation."

Sarah looked around; people were eating and chatting, obviously enjoying themselves.

"I understood that as all the tables are busy. A cup of coffee would be nice," Sarah said, and then smiled. "And maybe a small piece of French cake. I have a sweet tooth although, of course, I try to restrict my appetite because men prefer skinny ladies." Irony sparkled in her eyes behind those sunglasses.

"Sometimes I remind myself that we are what we eat," Jacob supported her, also a bit ironically. "Unfortunately I'm not Julius Caesar and cannot do two jobs simultaneously," he confessed. "The new file that Captain O'Burke has given me also interests me professionally."

He told Sarah about the O'Burke's task in great detail, and as well as the last conversation he had with his father.

Sarah smiled. "As I remembered, you were going to resign after you finished Rabbi Lieberman's case. Frankly, I doubt in that."

Jacob sighed. "Frankly, me too," he said. Then he told Sarah about his meeting Harold Fiedler, the lawyer for the 'Princess of Harlem.' "I realized that I wouldn't be able to work as a trial lawyer, Sarah. What else could I do?" He sighed. "But my father sees me a writer. Do you?"

"Your father is a sage, Jacob. If he sees you a writer, you can definitely be a writer. You have experience in investigation with a lot of mysterious criminal cases; each of them can be described as unique and worthy of a novel."

"We're talking too much about me, Sarah. What about you? Did you finish the 'Messiah's Coming'?"

"No," Sarah said frankly, but Jacob heard bitterness in her voice. "I doubt that I'll be able to finish it for some time. I sit in front of the canvas for hours, but, at the best, I can add one or two brush touches."

"Maybe it would make sense to put this work aside temporarily and concentrate on a new one."

Sarah took her glasses off and looked at Jacob carefully. He saw that her eyes were sad and tired.

"I cannot," she whispered. "I tried, but 'Messiah' takes all my energy. I cannot do anything else." Sarah put her glasses on again. "I'm going crazy, Jacob," she whispered, "I've destroyed all my other canvases."

"Have you destroyed all your wonderful paintings?" Jacob's eyes rolled up. He felt a lump in his throat.

"Yes, all but 'Messiah.' I think I was born to only paint that one picture."

"Maybe you need a vacation. Fly with me to Russia, Sarah. You must rest."

"I'm tempted, Jacob. Unfortunately, a new movie that I've worked on now is on the eve of being released. But if you make me a similar offer some other time, I wouldn't be able to refuse."

Sarah made an attempt to smile. She thought that she would not be able to refuse any other of Jacob's offer. But she knew that Jacob would not make that offer.

Jacob laid his hand over hers. "I don't agree with your spirit, Sarah. I know what you have to do - go to a synagogue and pray. Not for atonement because such a pure soul as yours need no atonement; for advice about how to express your feelings for God on canvas. Maybe you are the first Jewish painter who tries to do this. You try to reach perfection, but perfection is unreachable. You would never say to yourself 'it's perfect' although what you've done is already perfect. I want you to understand it. Torah says, *'don't try to understand...because it's beyond human understanding.'* You've already seen much deeper than all others; don't try to penetrate through the curtain. 'Messiah's Coming' is your masterpiece. It's done. You feel Messiah is coming, and He is coming. Will we be witnesses of His arrival? Maybe. Let's live and wait as if He is on the way. Live not for destruction, but for creation."

Jacob raised Sarah's hand and kissed it. When he looked at Sarah's face, he saw a tear running along her cheek.

20.

"Jack," said Captain O'Burke as he came to Jacob's office. "You need to get a refund for your ticket to Russia."

Jacob looked at him with surprise. "Why?"

"Norman Winder, the man you were going to talk to, doesn't work in St. Petersburg any more. The state department informed us that he was promoted to consul and transferred to Australia."

"Why?" Jacob asked again.

O'Burke grinned. "Your language could be richer. A promotion is a promotion."

"A position in Australia looks like a demotion," Jacob remarked thoughtfully.

"We don't work at the state department. I think they have different criteria. You can exchange your ticket and go to Melbourne."

"I don't like flying that much, captain; the way to Melbourne is twice as long. So I think I'll keep my ticket to Helsinki."

"Helsinki?"

"There is no direct flight to St. Petersburg from New York," Jacob explained, "only through Helsinki."

"What are you going to do in Russia if Norman Winder is in Australia? Take a guided tour of the Hermitage at the police department expense is a bad idea," Captain O'Burke said without a smile.

"It's a good idea, captain, and I'll definitely do as you advised.

After that, I'd like to visit Russian police headquarters. Since Russia joined the Interpol, I suppose they have to provide assistance for our investigation."

O'Burke thought few minutes. "Okay, Jack, I'll call our Interpol section and ask for the contact person in St. Petersburg." He paused on Jacob's office threshold. "Take the English-Russian phrase book with you; not everybody speaks English."

"Don't worry, captain. I can speak Yiddish too."

O'Burke grinned and left, closing the door behind him.

*

FinAir was the most convenient airline for Jack to take to St. Petersburg. The flight from New York to Helsinki took only seven hours. After a short wait, he was onboard another, smaller Boeing 727 that landed in St. Petersburg in less than an hour.

After Jacob passed through customs and was on his way to hire a taxi, he saw a man holding a sign with his name on it. Jacob walked over to him.

"Hi, I am Jacob Reterseil."

"Good day, sir," the man said in English with a strong

Russian accent. "Colonel Borisov asked me to meet you and deliver you to the hotel."

Colonel Borisov was the Interpol contact person that Captain O'Burke had mentioned to Jacob before his departure.

The man took Jacob's small traveling suitcase and escorted him to the black car with flashing lights on its roof that was standing near the airport entrance. Following the man, Jacob thought that you could always unmistakably identify people who belonged to the brotherhood of police persons.

"Hotel 'Europe,'" Jacob said as he sat on the back seat.

"I know, sir."

"Is it far from the center of the city?"

"It's strictly in the center, sir.'

The ride took about thirty minutes. Soon the car stopped in front of the entrance to a beautiful and impressive building.

"Here is your hotel, sir," said the man. "I think you'll enjoy your stay in our city."

The man carried Jacob's luggage to the desk. He waited until Jacob checked in and received the key from his room.

"Here is my phone, sir. If you need transportation, please give me a call. My name is Vitaly. Today is Friday. On Monday, Colonel Borisov would be glad to see you in his office. Enjoy your weekend, sir." Vitaly touched his temple with his hand as if he wore a uniform, and left.

Jacob took an elevator to the fifth floor and entered his room. Looking around, Jacob thought that the Russian hotel was obviously one of the best that he had stayed in; not worse than the Amsterdam Hilton.

Jacob rested a little, and then went downstairs to the winter garden café for a cup of coffee. At the far end of the garden, on a little stage, a trio – a violin, a cello, and a piano

– performed music by Vivaldi. He sat nearby and enjoyed the music. The faces of the three young ladies-musicians seemed beautiful to him. Art always makes people beautiful, Jacob thought as he remembered Sarah. But it also makes them unhappy as all of them try to penetrate to the world of perfection; and most of them fail. Jacob listened to the music for some time, then drank his coffee and returned to his room.

It was Friday, the Sabbath approached, and Jacob decided to visit a synagogue. From the guidebook, Jacob knew that the St. Petersburg synagogue was built in the nineteen century by one of the most influential and richest Russian Jews, Baron Hinzberg. It was considered one of the most beautiful synagogues in Europe, and now Jacob had a chance to see it.

Although Vitaly offered to be available for transportation any time, Jacob decided not to call him but to hire a taxi instead. As he went out the hotel, a taxi was waiting nearby. He got into the cab and handed a driver a guidebook that he had bought in New York.

"Ler-mon-tov-sky pros-pect," Jacob said, pronouncing the letters of the Slovenian language with great difficulty. Being unsure that the driver understood him, Jacob added, "the synagogue." Synagogue is synagogue in all languages, he thought.

"A synagogue?" the driver repeated with a scowl and an unpleasant tone. After he started up the engine, he added, "Twenty dollars."

Jacob knew it was too much, but he didn't argue and agreed. "Okay," he said.

Fifteen minutes later, the taxi stopped in front of a massive, iron gate. He paid his fare and stepped out of the cab.

Behind the gate, Jacob saw a magnificent building. To his surprise, the door of the synagogue was closed although the sun had just set. He looked around at a loss. Then he saw two old Jewish men who were going to the far end of the yard.

"Excuse me!" Jacob exclaimed. "I wonder if the synagogue is functioning."

"What is he talking about?" one old man asked the other in Yiddish.

Heard Yiddish, Jacob said 'Shabbat Shalom.' Then he repeated the question in Yiddish.

"Yes," one of the men said. "We have *minyan* in the small synagogue. Follow us."

Following the old men, Jacob climbed a narrow staircase to the second floor. He found himself in a small room where about a dozen people prayed. Another old man came to him, offering a *tales*. In the other hand he held a donation box. He said nothing, but his eyes clearly said that he expected a lavish donation from a foreigner. Jacob took a hundred dollar bill from his wallet and dropped it into the donation box. It was big money, and the old Jew giggled with satisfaction.

"I heard you spoke in Yiddish," he said.

"I did."

"Are you American?"

Jacob nodded.

"When I was young, I also dreamed to become an American. But some one must live here, in Russia. What's the difference? We all live in Diaspora until we move to Israel," the old man said thoughtfully. He stepped aside to the Western wall to pray.

Jacob also concentrated on the prayer, *"Baruch ata Adonay, Adonay elocheiny, Adonay echad; asher kidshany, bemitzvotav vetsivany, leadlik ner shel Shabbat kodesh."*

He prayed for some time, and then he went to the old man who offered him a *tales*.

"Would you show me the main synagogue, please?" he asked.

As the old Jew didn't respond immediately, Jacob gave him another hundred dollar bill.

"I will," the man agreed. He put the bill in his pocket, not in the donation box. "Follow me."

Jacob followed the old man to the main hall which was huge and decorated with rich window paintings.

"When do you open the main entrance?" Jacob asked.

"For the High Holiday season only," the old man said. "But now it's never full. Few Jews have remained in St. Petersburg; in the last thirty years, most of them had emigrated," he explained.

"How many Jews still live in St. Petersburg?"

"No more than several hundred families; at least those who identify themselves as Jews," he clarified. "The rest are assimilated Jews. They do not want to remember their predecessors. This is Russia; it was always not easy to be a Jew here," the old man said bitterly.

"It's not easy to be a Jew," Jacob agreed, leaving the synagogue.

When Jacob returned to the hotel, it was already late. He went to the restaurant for a late dinner, and then headed to his room. He switched on the TV and watched it for several minutes without sound. Then he switched it off. I need time to think over my upcoming conversation to Colonel Borisov, he thought, trying to concentrate on the Turnikov's case. But he wasn't in the mood to think about work. No work for today, he reminded himself. Shabbat has begun. So Jacob has changed his mind and went downstairs to the bar. Shabbat Shalom.

21.

On Monday morning, after he had a light breakfast, Jacob called Vitaly.

"This is Jacob Reterseil speaking."

"Good morning, sir. The car is waiting for you."

When Jacob went out, he saw the same black car near the hotel entrance. At seeing Jacob, Vitaly opened the car door for his passenger.

After the fifteen minutes ride along the beautiful streets of Old Petersburg, which reminded Jacob of Barcelona he had visited two years ago, the car stopped in front of a massive, gray building whose architecture was not in harmony with the surrounding buildings. Jacob would rather refer it architecture to a constructivist style, popular at the beginning of the twentieth century.

Accompanied by Vitaly, who now wore a police uniform with three small stars on his epaulettes, Jacob went to the officer sitting at a stand in the middle of the huge hall. The duty officer stood and saluted Vitaly as he had a higher rank officer. Vitaly spoke to him in Russian, put his signature in the journal that lay on the desk, and asked Jacob to show the duty officer his police ID. Then they took the elevator to the third floor.

The building and its atmosphere inside didn't look that of the U.S. police precincts with their open space, hubbub, telephone calls, and open interrogations. Jacob was surprised by deep silence around him. He saw no police officers, only a long row of closed doors in front of him. Jacob thought that this building reminded him of another building – the S.S. headquarters in Berlin. He had watched one of the Hollywood movies about WWII and he remembered it was a comedy.

"Is this police headquarters?" Jacob asked Vitaly as they approached one of those closed doors.

"The Russian police department is a part of the Ministry of Interior Affairs," Vitaly explained dryly as they reached one of the doors with a sign on it, *Colonel A. Borisov.*

Vitaly knocked. Then he opened the door and saluted Colonel Borisov from the threshold. After Jacob came in, Vitaly closed the portal behind them.

The man sitting at a large desk stood up with an open smile on his face. Then he went to Jacob to shake his hand.

"Welcome to Russia, detective," he said in perfect English, and invited Jacob to sit in one of the deep leather chairs in the corner of the room. "I am Alex Borisov," he said, not mentioning his rank.

Alex Borisov was about Jacob's age, even younger, with a pleasant, open face, and the clever eyes of a highly educated man. He didn't wear a uniform; his conservative, dark gray suit was, without a doubt, made in Italy.

"I'm Jacob Reterseil of NYPD," Jacob introduced himself. From his first glance, he liked Colonel Borisov. He didn't look like the KGB officers he had seen in the stereotyped

Hollywood movies. "Where did you study English, sir? Yours is more British than mine." Jacob smiled.

Colonel Borisov returned the smile. "I've graduated from St. Petersburg University, the Faculty of English Literature. Are you surprised?"

"Not at all." Jacob paused. Then he said, "You obviously know the reason of my visit to Russia. I'm trying to lift the curtain of mystery about the death of an American diplomat's daughter-in-law, who was a naturalized US citizen, but was born in Russia."

"I know what happened only in general, not specifics. As it happened in the U.S., the case is under your jurisdiction."

He took a box of Cuban cigars from a small table, opened it, and offered one to Jacob.

"Thank you, sir, but I don't smoke."

"If you don't object," Colonel Borisov said and lit a cigar, releasing a good portion of tobacco smoke.

"Let me share with you, colonel, our information on that case," Jacob said. "From our point of view, it was definitely a murder, not a suicide. The first question in such a case is usually was it sexual assault? The medical examiner's office gave a negative answer. The second question was whether it had been a robbery. The simple conclusion was no because nothing was removed from Mrs. Winder's body; no robber would neglect a $30,000 ring or $15,000 watch."

Jacob paused and looked carefully at Colonel Borisov. As the colonel kept silent, Jacob continued, "It was quite clear that the murder was a hint to attract somebody's attention. In such a case, whose? I'll be quite frank with you, colonel. I supposed it could be a matter of national security as Ana Winder was the daughter-in-law of an American diplomat. One of the versions was that it could have been the actions of the KGB, but neither the FBI nor the CIA had found something interesting in this case for them; they had cleared Norman Winder.

I think that we are dealing with some kind of criminal activity; but what kind? I'd like you, colonel, to help me find the answer to this question," Jacob concluded his tirade.

"I'm willingly to cooperate with you, detective, and provide all the information we have. What do you need?"

"I'd like to have information about all of Ana Winder's relatives who are still alive and live in Russia."

"I'll prepare it for you, detective, by tomorrow."

"It would be greatly appreciated, colonel.'

Colonel Borisov stood and shook Jacob's hand. He pressed a small knob on his table, and Vitaly instantaneously opened the door as if he had been standing behind the door, waiting for a call. His black car delivered Jacob back to the hotel.

"Enjoy your day, sir," he said and saluted Jacob, touching his hand to his police cap.

22.

The next day Jacob was working in Colonel Borisov's office.

"My office is at your disposal, Mr. Reterseil. I'll temporarily occupy the adjacent one," the colonel said as Jacob came to the room.

"Please call me Jacob, colonel. We Americans have gotten accustomed to a less formal work relationship." He smiled. "Or, if you're more comfortable with an English name, call me Jack."

"I'm quite comfortable with the name Jacob." Colonel Borisov smiled in return. "My wife has Jewish roots. I'll also be more comfortable if you call me Alex," he added.

Jacob worked with the documents for several hours, but found nothing among them that would attract his attention.

Ana Turnikov was born in a decent family. Her parents were people who were called in Russia *intelligencia* – highly educated, but low socially profiled people. Her mother, a nurse, had died a year before her own death. As Ana was the only child and had no other close relatives, no one was available to give any information about her past.

Things happen. She could have turned out to be at a wrong place at a wrong time, Jacob thought tiredly. But her jewelry wasn't taken. It meant only one thing – someone had sent a message. To whom? Jacob tangled in his thoughts.

Only two men had come into Ana's life for last years – her husband and her father-in-law. Jacob analyzed her life and that of her husband, Jerry Winder, scrupulously. They studied together, fell in love, married, and even worked at the same hospital after they became doctors. She gave birth to two of Jerry's children; a happy young family, Jacob remembered his impression that he had after his conversation with Jerry Winder.

Norman Winder, Ana's father-in-law, worked in Russia and didn't interfere in his son's life; they were not too close. One of Jacob's ideas was that Norman Winder could have been recruited by the KGB, and then had refused to cooperate. But neither the FBI nor the CIA had found anything compromising him. He was promoted to the rank of consul and transferred to Australia. His daughter-in-law's murder seemed to be a total surprise for him.

After Ana's mother's death, her only relative in Russia remained her father, Ivan Turnikov. But who would send such a terrible message to a poor Russian retiree? This was nonsense, Jacob decided. Then he closed the file and went to the adjacent office.

"Alex," he said as he sat down. "I've come to a dead end, and I'm ready to suppose that a crazy maniac, who was not interested in money, killed Ana Turnikov only because he was eager to kill somebody just then. As we Americans say, she was at a wrong place at a wrong time. Does that sound plausible to you?"

"Not much, Jacob. Any other versions?"

"I'm sorry to say no, Alex. If you don't have any other information than what you have given me, the case is closed."

Colonel Borisov looked at his watch. "It's lunch time, Jacob. Let's go downstairs to our cafeteria; you won't be disappointed."

*

A waitress, who looked more like a male police officer than a woman, took their orders and stepped aside.

"You know, Jacob, several years ago there was a dark time in Russian history. The Russian empire had collapsed, democracy still didn't exist, crime was up, and the criminal cartels controlled business and the economy. Robberies and murders were so frequent that, in many cases, the police was powerless," Colonel Borisov said in the informative manner.

"One of those cases was a robbery of the Russian Museum. Like the Hermitage, the Russian Museum holds our state art treasures. If the Hermitage's exhibitions include the world's art, the Russian Museum exhibits contains only Russian art – from Andrei Rublev's fourteenth century icons to Marc Chagall's pictures, and even canvases painted by famous Soviet art dissidents like Oscar Rabin. By the way, one of his pictures decorates the White House in your capital," Colonel Borisov explained as the artist's name was unfamiliar to Jacob. Then he took a gulp of soda and continued, "During the robbery, five canvases were stolen, two by Marc Chagall and three by Vasily Kandinsky. They were chosen for a temporary exhibition of Russian art to be shown in Paris, and had been moved from the main exposition hall to the basement level where security was not so strong. The market price of the stolen pictures was about ten millions dollars. If they were sold at one of the art auctions, it would have been much more." Colonel Borisov detected the range of interest in Jacob's eyes, and continued the story. "The thieves were never found, and the tracks of the stolen pictures vanished. We supposed they could have been driven to the West, and observed all art operations carefully; not only the Sothbey's and Christy's, but also Bonham's and McDouglas," Colonel Borisov said, showing he was not a novice in the art world.

After their lunch arrived, they ate silently for some time. Jacob was absorbing the information he had heard. Colonel Borisov did not interrupt his thoughts.

"Why Russia didn't initiate the Interpol investigation?" Jacob asked at last.

"The pictures were never sold, and we had come to the dead end in our investigation. Now there are as many very rich private collectors in Russia as in the West. Perhaps the canvases had never gone abroad, and some ego-maniac enjoys them in the basement of his castle." Colonel Borisov paused and poured a diet Pepsi into his glass. As Jacob didn't interrupt him and didn't ask questions, he took several gulps and continued, "Ivan Turnikov, as the curator of the museum's section where the stolen pictures had hung, was one of the suspects. But prosecution failed to prove his participation in crime. The robbery had occurred while he was visiting his daughter who lived in the U.S. She had given birth to Ivan Turnikov's second grandson. After the investigation was closed, the museum's administration forced Ivan Turnikov to resign. He was under observation for more than a year, but the police came to the final conclusion that he was clean.

This unlucky man had not only lost his job, but a year later his wife died from a heart attack. His life had brought to naught," Colonel Borisov completed his monologue and looked at Jacob.

"Of course, Alex, there is a chance that these canvases are still in one of the private Russian collections. I think the number of Russian billionaires will soon exceed the amount in the U.S. But usually the police know or guess who these people are," Jacob remarked.

"We also know our main private collectors, Jacob. Forty years ago I would have even suggested that it was Mr. Uri Andropov's order that removed these pictures from the museum." Colonel Borisov smiled cunningly. "He had the largest private collection of abstract art in the USSR.," he explained. "In today Russia, I know that Mr. Putin is not a collector."

Jacob thought their conversation was frank; they were talking not in the colonel's office. A half-empty cafeteria was a safer place to talk.

"I doubt that the canvases are still in Russia," Jacob said thoughtfully. "If they had reached their destination to one of the private Russian collections, there would be no sense in murdering Ana Turnikov in the U.S. But she was murdered. Now I'm assured that Ivan Turnikov was definitely involved in the robbery of the Russian Museum."

Colonel Borisov peered at Jacob. "What was his motive for that robbery?" he asked. "Not profit as after the robbery Ivan Turnikov has lived the life of a half-beggar and physically ill man; if not profit, what else?"

"That is a good question, Alex. I think something went wrong with the projected plan; either the canvases didn't reach the addressee or the thieves weren't paid for the job.

Ana Winder's murder could be a hint to only one man – her father. I would even suggest that it was he who had organized the robbery."

"We have interrogated Ivan Turnikov many times, but he fiercely denied any participation in that robbery," Colonel Borisov remarked.

"The Russian juridical system is too strict," Jacob said. "Mr. Turnikov knew that if he had confessed, he would be imprisoned for a long time. You don't have at your disposal, Alex, such a nice juridical invention as 'plea bargain,' that can grant immunity from prosecution, or a 'witness protection program.' He denied his involvement in the robbery, but now many changes have happened in his life. His partners have killed his wife and his daughter; he knows he'll be next."

"Your scheme, Jacob, is based on your assurance that the paintings have gone to the West. Even in the dark time of Russian history, after the collapse of the Soviet Empire, it wasn't easy to get through customs. But one way has always existed – diplomatic mail."

"Bingo, Alex! We have tied the knot. Norman Winder, Ivan Turnikov's new relative, could have been the man he needed. As the U.S. Vice-Consul in St. Petersburg, he could easily send the canvases abroad by a diplomatic mail."

"He would never confess in any illegal actions," Colonel Borisov remarked thoughtfully.

"He would, but only in one case – if Mr. Ivan Turnikov signs a full confession that would be shown him as a part of an Interpol investigation. But now, Alex, I'd like us to both interrogate Ivan Turnikov. If he's not an idiot, he will open his mouth."

"He will," Colonel Borisov agreed. "But before we do

this, let me exhume his wife's body. I need the medical examiner's office conclusion about her forcible death." Then he changed the topic. "I think our business day was fruitful enough. I know one place that's worth visiting for dinner in the evening. Will you object to relying on my taste, Jacob?" He smiled friendly.

"I won't, Alex," Jacob reassured him, returning the smile.

23.

Three days later Colonel Borisov, at Jacob's presence, interrogated a tall, skinny man with a tired face and dead eyes.

"Take a seat, Mr. Turnikov," Colonel Borisov said as the man entered his office. "We invited you for a conversation. This is not a formal interrogation. I'm Colonel Borisov," he introduced himself.

"What's the subject of our talk?" the man asked nervously, and looked at Jacob who sat silently.

"You know the topic, Mr. Turnikov. It's the Russian Museum robbery that took place about two years ago. Is there something you'd like to come right out and say?"

"No, not at all," Ivan Turnikov said quickly. Then he added, "The case is closed. I am clean." He shifted in his chair uncomfortably.

"Two years is a long time, Mr. Turnikov," Colonel Borisov said calmly. "Many things have happened here, in Russia, and in the U.S. Now this case is under the Interpol investigation. Its representative Detective NYPD Jacob Reterseil will also take part in our conversation. As he doesn't speak Russian,

I'll translate his questions and your answers for him. Let me emphasize again that it's not a formal interrogation, and a tape recorder is not on; it will be switched on only with your permission."

"I don't care," Ivan Turnikov said, not naturally. "I'm innocent."

Colonel Borisov paid no attention to his remark. He watched as Ivan Turnikov struggled to control his temper.

"Two members of your family have died because of you, Mr. Turnikov," he continued, "and I wouldn't give a poor Russian ruble for your life. What's the sense of your covering for people who murdered your wife and daughter?"

"Only God knows when death comes, colonel." Ivan Turnikov sighed. "My wife had a heart attack; my daughter's death was an accident as the American authorities informed me."

"In both cases you are wrong, Mr. Turnikov," Colonel Borisov said calmly. He looked without a blink into Ivan Turnikov's eyes. "Here is the final conclusion from the medical examiner's office after your wife's body was exhumed." He took a paper from the file in front of him and handed it to Ivan Turnikov.

As Ivan Turnikov read it, his fingers trembled visibly. He held the paper in front of his eyes much longer than necessary to read it. He looked crestfallen.

"As a diabetic, your wife used insulin on a daily bases. Some one 'helped her' inject a dose several times exceeding her norm. Regarding your daughter's death, Detective Reterseil has informed me that it was also a murder. Her death was a hint to someone. And we all know who that 'someone' is. Your wife is dead, your daughter is dead; who will be next, Mr. Turnikov, you or maybe your grandchildren?"

Colonel Borisov paused, and then translated his monologue to Jacob who was silent, studying Ivan Turnikov's face.
Then he switched on the recorder with the words, 'from your
permission, Mr. Turnikov.'

"I really do not know exactly what happened." Ivan
Turnikov sighed deeply. His voice trembled.

"Mr. Turnikov, you have suffered enough and we,
Detective Reterseil and I, don't want to increase your suffering. The detective persuaded me to offer you 'a plea bargain'
as the Americans call such an agreement. You provide us with
all the information you know and sign a full confession; we,
in our turn, will grant you full immunity from prosecution.
I've already coordinated this deal with the district attorney."
Colonel Borisov made a pause, but Ivan Turnikov kept
silent. "You are a clever man, Mr. Turnokov, and have to
understand that only your full cooperation can save your life;
and maybe the lives of your grandchildren in the U.S.," the
colonel added.

"They'll kill me at any case," Ivan Turnikov said hoarsely,
trying to clear his throat.

"Who are *they*?" The colonel leaned forward, just
slightly.

"I don't know. I've dealt with only one man who introduced himself as Victor Romanovich; an old man, about
seventy, with a gray bead and intelligent face." Ivan Turnikov
sighed as he recollected the face. "He came to my office in
the museum and said that they knew about the upcoming
exhibition in Paris. He handed me a list of the canvases to be
added to the pictures that were already chosen for the exhibition; two canvases by Marc Chagall, and three by Vasily
Kandinsky. I told him the pictures were already selected, but
he smiled and said that it was never too late to earn $50,000. I

was surprised, and asked the man what he was talking about. Then he explained that my job would be easy – just to give him a drawing with the museum basement's security. He persuaded me that I would be beyond suspicion, as they would take the pictures out when I would be on vacation. While I hesitated, he smiled and added that he would increase this amount to $100,000. For that I only needed to persuade my American relative Norman Winder in sending the canvases abroad by diplomatic mail. 'We are not cheap and very reliable people,' he said."

Suddenly Ivan Turnikov put his head down on his arms and cried. When he raised his head, his eyes were full of tears of desperate. The colonel handed him a glass of water. He drank, wiped his tears and sighed. After a pause he continued, "I went to Norman Winder and offered him $50,000 for his help. He agreed quickly, but requested a $10,000 down payment. Victor Romanovich didn't object. He brought me money, and I gave them Mr. Winder." Ivan Turnikov stopped talking and lifted his desperate eyes on silent Jacob. He asked another glass of water and drank it in one gulp. Then he finished, "I don't know what happened, but Mr. Winder didn't bring me the canvases in the U.S. I begged him, but he said that, obviously, something had happened with the mail as he had never received it." Ivan Turnikov paused deeply.

Colonel Borisov translated his words to Jacob.

"Tell him, Alex, that I'll do my best to force Norman Winder to return the pictures," Jacob remarked.

After Ivan Turnikov signed his confession, Colonel Borisov said, "If Victor Romanovich, although I doubt this is his real name, calls you, please let us know immediately. Sooner or later we'll find him and his gang. As soon as we return pictures to the Russian Museum, your nightmare will be finished and your life will be beyond danger, Mr. Turnikov."

After the colonel signed Ivan Turnikov's pass and he left, the colonel turned to Jacob. "What's your opinion, Jacob?"

"He told the truth, Alex, I think Norman Winder's greediness had killed Ivan Turnikov's wife and daughter. He realized that he would earn much more if he had kept the pictures and sold them later on himself. But I think they're still in his possession. He hadn't time to find a private collector who would be interested to buy the paintings, and he is, obviously, a very prudent person. But punishing him won't be too easy. Although he has violated Russian laws, an attempt at his formal extradition, even based on Ivan Turnikov's confession, would be useless, taking into account his diplomatic immunity. Our American juridical system gives a big advantage to convicting a suspect based on the confession of only one witness, although it strictly contradicts Moses' law." As Colonel Borisov looked at him questioningly, Jacob explained, "Moses wrote that in such situations, no one could be convicted. As an example, the former U.S. Attorney Rudy Guliani had made his career when he sent one of the bosses of New York Mafia to jail. His prosecution was based on the confession of a serial killer, who was already sentenced to many life terms and was ready to sign anything if it could make his life easier. It was a judicial nonsense," Jacob repeated. Then he changed the point. "I'll fly to Australia, and I think I'll take this man. We'll return the stolen pictures to the Russian Museum, Alex." He stood up and extended his hand to Colonel Borisov.

"You know, Jacob, it was not just a great pleasure to work with you," Colonel Borisov said sincerely. "You have broken the thin ice of my prejudices against Americans, who are supposed to be our enemies as we were taught since childhood. I do hope your short stay in St. Petersburg was pleasant. If you come to Russia again, maybe with your wife, please let me know beforehand. I'll do my best to open Russian gates wider for you."

"I'm divorced, Alex." Jacob said casually.

"In that case, maybe you'll find a new wife here. You may have noticed that Russian women are beautiful." Colonel Borisov smiled softly.

"It's hardly to be expected, Alex," Jacob returned him a sad smile. "I am a Jew, and would like to marry a Jewish woman. But as an old man in the St. Petersburg synagogue told me, only several hundred families in the city still identify themselves Jews."

"We live in Russia," Colonel Borisov said indefinitely, and Jacob didn't quite catch what he had in view.

"I'll keep you informed, Alex, about any further developments," he said as Colonel Borisov showed him to the door and they shook hands.

24.

On the FinAir plane on the way home, Jacob found his seat near a middle-aged man with an intelligent face and clever eyes. The bold dome of his head was ringed with long gray hair falling to his shoulders. He wore a short Hemingway style beard, and Jacob, not instantly, paid attention to the Orthodox Christian cross on a lapel of his jacket. The man turned out to be an Orthodox Russian priest. Having seen a *kipa* on Jacob's head, the man smiled.

"I think it would be my pleasure to chat with a rabbi if you don't mind. The flight is long. Let me introduce myself, I'm Father Gregory."

"I'm Jacob. But I must disappoint you, sir; I'm not a rabbi."

Father Gregory smiled. "But you are a Jew, an elder and beloved brother of Christians."

Jacob laughed. "Under such an angle…"

After the plane had reached its cruising altitude and the flight attendant served a light snack, Father Gregory said, "Mr. Jacob, I think you share my view that there are no accidental events in our world, and every meeting in our life is forecast from Above."

"I do," Jacob agreed and looked at Father Gregory carefully.

"I think God sent you to me to dispel some of my doubts," Father Gregory said frankly. "I met you, sir, for the first and, obviously, the last time in my life. That's why I can be so frank with you and with myself." He paused. Jacob did not interrupt him. Father Gregory looked at Jacob's face openly. "For some time I've been thinking that we Christians trust in a man-made god. When we discarded the First Commandment, we created a new religion. But a true religion cannot be created by man, only by God. What did God give to people? The Torah. That means that only Judaism remains the true religion." Father Gregory sighed deeply. "For many years we tried to kill Judaism, and it was the greatest sin before God," he said emotionally.

Jacob looked at the man's face very carefully. "I don't know what to say, Mr. Gregory. Every Jew considers Judaism to be the only true religion; like every Christian considers Christianity the same," he added diplomatically. Then, after a pause, he asked carefully, "Excuse me, Mr. Gregory, but what caused doubts in your faith?"

"Frankly, the first nail in the coffin of my doubts was hammered when I read about the recent scientific definition of the Torino Coat's age. It keeps the tracks of Christ's body, so the coat's age supposed to be dated back to the first century. But the using of the radio-carbonic method of age definition had referred us to the period of XI-XIII centuries. In this case Christianity didn't exist until the end of the first Millennium of our era; that is nonsense." Father Gregory paused, expecting Jacob's questions. As Jacob kept silent, he continued thoughtfully, "If the Torino Coat is not a fake, I have to ask myself a question at what time Christ lived or he didn't live but was invented?" He looked at Jacob as he wanted to read the answer on his face.

"As I know, Mr. Gregory, the radiological methods of estimating ages of the archeological subjects have huge errors," Jacob said. "For example the age of shell of an American mollusk living today was defined as 1200 years old. I think if your doubts are based only on age definition by modern physics..."

"I have made my own research," Father Gregory said quietly. "It connected with the new star born on the East. We Christians consider it had place when Christ was born. And then, thirty-one years later, there had been the full sun eclipse in Palestine when Christ was reborn. I have checked all known star atlases, old and new. I found that such a rare event as a full star eclipse had never place in the first century in Palestine. It had place only in the eleventh century, and not in Palestine but in the Mediterranean. How could I not to ask a question when Christ was born and what is the Christianity?" Father Gregory's monologue looked like a confession, and Jacob didn't interrupt him. It was too a personal matter to discuss. "What is Christianity? Father Gregory repeated the question to himself. "It has too many branches: Orthodox, Catholic, Protestant, Mormon, not counting of hundreds of different cults and groups. Man can interpret everything but religion." The intensity of Father Gregory's emotion began to grow.

"Christian theology accepts that Judaism is the basis for Christianity," Jacob said carefully as he hadn't yet caught the direction of Father Gregory's thoughts.

Gregory looked at Jacob but didn't respond to his remark.

"To believe means to accept," he said thoughtfully. "You know, Mr. Jacob, what confuses me is that Judaism is also not a monolithic religion. If it were given by God, today it has to remain in the same form that was given by God thousands years ago. But what is Judaism today? Secular Judaism, Orthodox Judaism, Conservative Judaism, and Reform Judaism … Can you explain the difference between them? Can we call Judaism the true religion today?"

"You know, Mr. Gregory, I'm afraid it wouldn't be easy for me to give the answer to your question. I was born in an Orthodox family. All Orthodox Jews believe that God gave the entire Torah to Moses on Mount Sinai in two parts – the written Torah that contains 613 *mitzvot*, and the spoken Torah, the oral traditions and explanations later recorded in the work of the sages of the Talmud."

"As I understand it, being a Jew means accepting God as the creator of the Torah. Am I right?" Father Gregory asked.

Jacob smiled. "I think to this day there's less agreement among even Orthodox Jews about what being Orthodox means – especially about how particular laws should be followed – than there is disagreement in any other modern movement. For example, the state of Israel has not one but two 'chief' rabbis; one is chosen to serve the Ashkenazi, who developed in Europe, and another one the Sephardic, who developed in what today are primarily Arab lands."

"I am trying to find an analogy in the development of our beliefs, Mr. Jacob. Revised Orthodox Christianity created Catholicism; reformed Catholicism had led us to Protestantism. I can understand Reform Catholicism, but I cannot understand what Reform Judaism mean."

His question remained without an answer.

"Ladies and Gentlemen, this is the captain's speaking. Because of turbulence ahead, please fasten your belts," they heard the captain's voice interrupt them. Then they felt vibration of the plane's body.

Jacob wasn't airsick, but he felt uncomfortable. He asked the attendant for a glass of water. As she brought it, he looked at her face, which was calm and impenetrable. If she knew we were going to die soon, her face would keep the same, trained expression, he thought.

Jacob closed his eyes. The plane shook again. What had the Russian priest asked him? What was Reform Judaism? He had never thought about it much. What stupid words, Reform Judaism! How could a religion that was given by God be reformed by humans?

The turbulence lasted only a short time. When Jacob opened his eyes, Father Gregory smiled. "Are you okay, Mr. Jacob?"

"I'm fine. Are you?"

"Before I had come to Christianity and was ordained, I served in the Air Force," he said with a tiny smile.

"Did you?" Jacob's surprise was sincere.

"After my military service, I entered aviation school because I had dreamed of becoming a pilot," Father Gregory said casually. "But my dream didn't come true."

"Why?" Jacob asked. "Excuse my curiosity, sir," he added.

Father Gregory sighed. "While one of the training flights, a friend of mine had died," he said quietly. He paused for a long time. "His parachute was damaged," he explained, then added, "It was really my parachute; he gave me his own to save my life." A long silence came as he had pondered the events of the past. "God had chosen another way for me." Father Gregory waved to the stewardess and ordered a cognac. "Will you have a drink with me, Mr. Jacob, to my friend's memory?"

"I will." Jacob nodded.

After they drank, Father Gregory smiled. "The charm of the past is in the past," he said. "I asked you, Mr. Jacob, about Reform Judaism. Don't be surprised at my interest in Judaism. You may not believe it, but my daughter is married to a Jewish man. I'm on my way to visit her in New York. You know, she is not only married to a Jew, but she has become a Jewish woman. Only God knows our ways." He sighed again.

"Reform Judaism?" Jacob repeated. "Reform Jews believe that the Torah was written and edited by human beings, though some profess the belief that the Ten Commandments were written by Moses and given to the people at Mount Sinai. Nonetheless, Reform Jews generally believe that the Torah and its ideas were inspired. I should say, Reform Jews are required to study as much as possible and do make intelligent choices based on what they learned. I think that sharing this point of view, we would come to the conclusion that Judaism is another man-made religion. In this case, it doesn't differ from Christianity. Are you, Mr. Gregory, particularly interested in Reform Judaism because your daughter had married a Reform Jew?"

"I don't know if my son-in-law is a Reform Jew, although he doesn't wear a yarmulke as you do. But his family is conservative. It was his family who insisted on my daughter going through all the procedures to become a Jewish woman."

"Did she go through the *giur*?"

"Yes. I had forgotten that word, *giur*. Now she is more Jewish than her husband," Father Gregory said.

"If your son-in-law's family belongs to Conservative Judaism, they believe that some kind of Divine revelation took place at Mount Sinai. Some maintain that the written Torah was given to Moses; others agree that the Torah was the work of human hands.

I was born in a Hassidic family. Hassidic Judaism, like Orthodox Christianity, demands complete faith. It is probably vestigial – the last gasp of a movement that brought new vigor to the Jewish world. Ironically, early Hassidism was the exact opposite of present day Hassidism. It set out to be a liberal influence in the Jewish world." Jacob smiled and looked at his watch.

"Our flight is almost done. Are your doubts dispelled, Mr. Gregory?"

"Pretty much, Mr. Jacob," Father Gregory said, removing a cross from the lapel of his jacket and slipping it into his pocket. As he caught Jacob's surprising look, he smiled. "No, I am not going to be converted to Judaism. My daughter doesn't like having a cross in her house, and I respect her wishes. I'm not able to accept Judaism," he explained, "as there are too many Christian dogmas in my attic." He touched the side of his head. "But I definitely know that I won't be able to perform my duties as a priest of the Russian Orthodox Church any more; I have accepted the First Commandment as the main one – the Lord is One. If you ask me, Mr. Jacob, where I am now in my beliefs, I'm afraid I wouldn't be able to give you an answer. Sometimes I ask myself that question, maybe one day all people would trust in One God, and we would stop talking about such nonsense as the reformation of our faith. I am not a Christian in the orthodox meaning, and I'm not a Jew. Who am I? I'm one of those men who trust in God," Father Gregory said as if he were talking to himself. He looked in the window. "We're approaching the airport." He buckled up.

After the plane landed, Father Gregory turned to Jacob. "It was a great pleasure to talk to you, sir."

"Pleasure was mine, sir. I wish you the best, Mr. Gregory. The world is close, and maybe one day we'll meet each other again." Jacob smiled, heading out.

25.

"**D**ad, I'm back!" Jacob said as he made the first call after leaving JFK airport. "I've missed you."

"I've missed you too, son." Moses smiled in the receiver. "Are you okay?"

"I'm fine. I'm on my way to the office, and then I'll come by your place for lunch."

"I'll be waiting for you, son." Moses hung up.

*

When Jacob went to Captain O'Burke's office in police headquarters, the captain saw immediately that Jacob was in good spirits.

"I see, Jack, that you had a nice vacation." He grinned. "Your face tells me you didn't spend too much time in the office and enjoyed your stay in Russia."

"I really did, captain," Jacob agreed. "I haven't yet prepared my written report as I'm just off the plane, but if you are curious about the results of my business trip, I can inform you verbally."

"I'm not a curious man, Jack, but success is written on your face. They say a shared success is twice as pleasant." Captain O'Burke gestured Jacob to a chair.

He sat down and informed the captain about the results of his trip.

"Having Mr. Ivan Turnikov's recorded and visual confession, I think I'll be able to press Mr. Norman Winder for a plea bargain if you, captain, give me such authorization. We'll return the stolen paintings to the Russian Museum. But for this final kick, I have to fly to Australia. And to tell you the truth, captain, I'm not happy about it; I hate long flights," Jacob said, summing up his information.

Captain O'Burke chuckled. "Jack, frankly, I'm not happy with your flamboyant travels; I'm sure I won't be able to avoid some questions from the Comptroller's office. But taking into account the results, even if you ask me for a first class air ticket, I wouldn't refuse you. I'll talk to Assistant DA about a plea bargain authorization for Norman Winder. Enjoy your trip to Australia, and don't miss the opportunity to hunt an antelope. They say it's exciting."

"Captain, you forgot I'm a Jew. We don't kill animals."

"What about humans?"

"Very seldom; only humans who deserve to die."

Captain O'Burke smiled. "This is the reason that the State of Israel is shrinking," he grinned.

"That's right. Jewish liberalism doesn't allow killing people, but easily can kill society." Jacob agreed. "It kills everything except the trust in God," he said, terminating the conversation.

*

It was almost four o'clock when Jacob reached Moses' house and embraced his father. Then he kissed Bertha, who grumbled about the "poor traveler" while setting the table.

Jacob told Moses shortly about the results of his trip to Russia and his impressions.

"It turned out to be a beautiful country," Jacob said, summing up his story. "My prejudices about the country and its people were wrong. My trip was interesting, but it was, first of all, work. And the job is only half done; to finish it, I have to fly to Australia." Jacob looked at Moses carefully. "While in Australia, I intend to see Rabbi Korinetz."

Moses sighed. "You haven't yet discarded, son, your thoughts to bring him to justice? The more I think about it, the more I'm assured that he didn't deserve man's punishment. He is a man of pure soul."

"When did you come to that conclusion, dad?'

"Since I began my correspondence to him, I knew him better. But I was assured of it when you told me your tale, Jacob. He has done nothing wrong."

"But Rabbi Lieberman had died," Jacob objected weakly.

"Rabbi Lieberman had died because of God's will. All of us die because of His will; like Dr. Brodsky, who died three days ago." Moses said and sighed.

"Sarah's father died?" Jacob's brow rose in surprise.

"It was a heart attack. At our age things can happen any day."

"I didn't know about it and haven't yet expressed Sarah my condolences," Jacob said.

"You will. She is sitting *shiva* in her father's house, not far from here."

A long silence descended. Then Jacob said, "I have to see Rabbi Korinetz, dad. I have to talk to him despite the fact that I cannot, and would never be able to penetrate the *Kabbalah* on your or his level. Can you arrange my meeting him while I'm in Australia?"

"I think I can, son, but I object strongly to any of your actions that could bring him harm. Strongly object," Moses repeated, and looked at Jacob carefully.

They finished lunch in silence as if a black cat had run between them. At last Jacob wiped his mouth.

"I have to go to Sarah's place," he said, standing up. In the door he turned to Moses, "I have to talk to Rabbi Korinetz, dad. It's beyond me. But I promise not to forget that I, first of all, your son, not a police officer."

26.

With months, correspondence between Moses and Rabbi Korinetz had become far from the formal exchange of letters. Although both men had never seen each other, they felt mutual sympathy. It was based not only on common points of the special interest in *Kabbalah,* but on deep intellect and modesty. It couldn't be still called friendship, but it was already more than usual, formal acquaintance.

Moses didn't forget Jacob's words he was first of all his son, and in the depth of his soul hoped that Jacob's meeting with Rabbi Korinetz would finally change his attitude to the Rabbi Lieberman's death.

Firstly Moses intended to write Rabbi Korinetz a detailed letter, but then he had changed his mind as he still felt not too comfortable with his participation in Jacob's mission. Maybe he would give him a call later on, he decided. So he had sent a short one.

Dear Rabbi Korinetz:

As you recommended, I've read the last edition of Zohar that you sent me. I think we are getting closer to understanding the possibility of the transfusion of souls. God has hinted that everything is possible in His creation. It's only a matter of time when one of the sages proves that the spiritual aspect of human existence can define our physical existence. Again, thank you for the advice.

Using that case, I want to ask you to do me a favor. My son Jacob is going to visit Australia, and it would be greatly appreciated if you give him the opportunity for a conversation. He is collecting information for a book about the history of Orthodox Judaism, and your help in advising him would be difficult to overestimate.

Always Yours,
Dr. Moses Reterseil

Rabbi Korinetz' response was prompt.

Dear Dr. Reterseil:

I would be honored if you visited my house, but while it's too difficult for you to make such a long trip, be assured that it will be my pleasure to see your son in my house. It's big enough to provide him with hospitality. So if he doesn't object, he can stay at my place for as long as he wants.

Very truly yours,
Rabbi Avraham Korinetz

Dear Rabbi Korinetz:

My son Jacob will be in Australia in two weeks and, with your kind permission, will be in touch with you.

Using that case, I'll send with him a short synopsis of my unfinished book, under the working title 'The Rise of Political Zionism in Western Europe.' It would be greatly appreciated if you express your opinion about the German-Jewish philosopher Moses Mendelssohn, who stood for the possibility that a pious Jew could legitimately study and profit from the thoughts and literature of gentile Europe without loosing his own traditional Jewish values.

Very truly yours,
Dr. Moses Reterseil.

27.

When Jacob knocked on the front door, Sarah met him on the threshold. Jacob embraced her warmly, and she sobbed quietly against his shoulder.

"I didn't know," he said. "My dad has just told me today." He carefully avoided the word 'condolence,' feeling it would be too formal.

Sarah showed him to the living room. "I'll set up the table for a tea," she said quietly, and went to the kitchen.

Jacob looked around at numerous family photos on the walls. He thought it would be difficult for Sarah to stay alone in the house that featured the spirit of her father. Things happen, he thought and sighed. Death is natural, but relatives of dead people can never put up with this thought.

When Sarah was back with the tea trolley, she said as if she had read his thoughts, "When parents get old, we think we're prepared for their departure one day. But we never are. Only after my dad's death, did I realize what I had lost. Advancing in years, we do not become cleverer; rather we become more alone."

"You aren't the only daughter, are you?"

"I have an older brother. He, like my father, is a doctor. He lives with his family in Texas. But we aren't very close," Sarah said frankly.

Jacob tried to swallow the bad taste in his mouth. It was the same taste he had felt when his mother died. Although more than twenty years had passed, he couldn't forget the feeling of emptiness that was then born in his heart. And guilt that he could do nothing to minimize her sufferings: she had a lung cancer although she died from a heart attack.

Jacob looked at Sarah's face. What could he say to this woman sitting in front of him, the woman who had become his close friend?

They were drinking tea in silence, both submerged in the same thoughts. To break the silence, Jacob asked, "How is your 'Messiah's Coming'?"

"I'm free of it," Sarah said without emotion. Then she looked at him and explained, "I donated the picture to my synagogue."

"That was the best decision," Jacob approved. "Now you can go onward. You are a talented artist, Sarah."

"I must go further," she agreed. "Life's going on. The only question is where to?" she asked bitterly.

"Only God knows where we are going to," Jacob said thoughtfully. "I'm more than assured He'll show you the way."

She changed the topic of the conversation. "How was your trip to Russia?"

"I can say nothing about the country, but St. Petersburg is a wonderful city," Jacob said. Then he told Sarah about the results of his stay. "The people that I dealt with were far from the stereotypes I had of them," he said, summing up his tale.

"Time changes everything, even people's psychology," Sarah remarked thoughtfully. "Such rough and open anti-Semitism that our predecessors experienced in Russia went into the past, but I don't think the psychology of the nation could be changed totally. There was too much Jewish blood on Russian and Ukrainian hands in the past."

"It's easy to recollect on what hands there was no Jewish blood," Jacob remarked. "But I'd like you to visit Russia one day. Ignoring the issue of the people, the architecture is beautiful."

"Not to speak about the people," Sarah agreed. "Anyway are you soon flying to Australia?"

"As soon as possible. Not only to help in returning the pictures to the Russian Museum and close the case of a poor Russian girl murdered in New York. I'm eager to see the man who was the culprit of Rabbi Lieberman's death. He attracts me like a snake attracts a rabbit, excuse me for such a stupid comparison. Not he personally, but the force of his intellect," Jacob explained. "I think he is, at least, a leg ahead of all living beings in understanding God's creation."

"What reason will you use to get in touch with him?" she asked.

"In his correspondence with the rabbi, my father introduced me as a writer who collects documents about the history of Orthodox Judaism."

"It's plausible," Sarah agreed, "but I don't see under what pretext you are able to bring up Rabbi Lieberman's death."

"Frankly, I don't have the slightest idea." Jacob sighed. "Everything depends on the situation. I never predict anything; maybe God will give me a hint," Jacob said and he stood up. "Thank you for tea. Be strong, Sarah, and don't forget that I'm your friend that you can rely on."

"I don't."

Jacob gave Sarah a hug. "Be strong," he repeated, kissing her cheek. "Life is going on."

28.

Within two days Jacob was again onboard a plane. This flight seemed long – it lasted almost twenty-four hours. There were only several passengers in business class, and nobody deflected Jacob from his thoughts. He tried to concentrate on the upcoming conversation with Rabbi Korinetz, but could not. More and more he came to the conclusion that the rabbi could be indicted for nothing. Can you blame a scientist when his assistant dies as a result of an unsuccessful experiment? In that case, why was he flying to Australia? The easy part of his job was to receive Consul Winder's confession. The man was done; his confession was only a formality. And a flight is only a reason to meet the rabbi. What would Jacob's conversation with the rabbi change? Could he expect the rabbi to tell him the discovery of the soul transfusion? Jacob caught the thought that he would be ready to take part in the new rabbi's experiment, even if it jeopardized his own life. It would be nice to receive a new, pure soul and not to carry the heavy burden of his entire life list of mistakes and omissions. But he remembered Moses' words that participating in such an experiment as soul transfusion would require that both souls be equally pure. Alas, his soul was not suitable for the rabbi. In such a case, why was he so keen to see this man? He felt the force from Above, pushing him in that direction; he could not resist.

To discard those thoughts, Jacob opened the book that his father had given him and tried to concentrate on it. Reading, to his surprise, he suddenly heard the stewardess say, "Ladies and gentlemen, please buckle your seat belts. We're approaching the Sydney airport. The temperature outside is sixty-seven degrees; there is a light rain."

*

The American Consulate in Sydney occupied a small two-story building, and it didn't impress Jacob. He thought that, in comparison to the American consulate in St. Petersburg, wonderful, old palace in the center of St. Petersburg that belonged to one of the Russian princes before the Bolshevik Rebellion, the Sydney Consulate building looked too provincial.

Was Norman Winder's new position promotion or banishment? Jacob grinned, entering the consulate. Jacob went to the administrative assistant's desk. A lady of indefinite age and an indifferent expression on her wrinkled face raised her eyes on him silently.

"I'd like to see Mr. Norman Winder," he said casually.

"Do you have an appointment, sir?" Her Australian accent was heavy, but it was still English.

"No, but it would be nice if he finds a few minutes for me."

"Your name, sir?"

Jacob took his business card out of his pocket and put it

on her desk. The woman looked at it, and surprise reflected in her eyes.

"Please have a seat, sir, while I contact the consul." She took Jacob's card and went to the door behind her desk, closing it carefully after she entered.

Several minutes later she was back with words, "Unfortunately, sir, the consul is busy now. But he will see you as soon as he is free."

"Okay, I'll wait," Jacob agreed, lowering his body into a chair.

Jacob guessed that Norman Winder needed time to prepare himself for a conversation with a NYPD detective. He definitely had to know that the conversation would be about his daughter-in-law's death in New York.

Jacob opened his briefcase. His glance stopped on *Zohar*. This book used to give him food for thoughts. But today his thoughts were heading in another direction. He took *The Times* off and looked it through for several minutes.

Jacob gave Norman Winder at least fifteen minutes to pretend to be busy. And he was right; at the fifteen minute mark, the secretary's phone rang. She picked up the receiver. "The consul is waiting for you, sir," she said.

When Jacob entered the consul's office, Norman Winder greeted him from behind the large desk. He pointed to a chair.

"Can I be useful to you, detective?" Norman Winder asked, trying to keep an indifferent tone in his voice.

Jacob sat and glanced at the man sitting in front of him. Norman Winder looked like a typical American bureaucrat. He appeared to be of British descent. He was swarthy, about fifty-five, had hair still naturally dark and brooding eyes that gave his face the cynical expression of a man who assured himself of more influence than he really had. He was of medium weight, perfectly shaved, with wire-rimmed glasses. After the first meeting, it would be difficult to recollect him the next day.

"I think you can, Mr. Winder," Jacob said, looking at the man's face.

"In what way, detective?"

"Be frank in answering my questions, Mr. Winder."

"What about?" Norman Winder tilted his head. "What do you have in view, detective?"

"Try to recollect everything that's connected with the death of your daughter-in-law, sir."

Norman Winder extended his hands. "Sorry, detective, but everything I know is that it was a tragic accident. This case was closed about half a year ago."

"It wasn't an accident, Mr. Winder; and the case was reopened at the Russians' request through the Interpol."

"If it wasn't an accident, what was it?" Norman Winder asked as if he had missed Jacob's remark about reopening the case.

"Murder, sir."

Norman Winder laughed. "That's nonsense. The NYPD had informed me that it wasn't either robbery or sexual assault. In such a case, how it could be a murder? How many senseless murder cases have you investigated, detective?"

"None. And your daughter-in-law's murder wasn't senseless, Mr. Winder. It was a hint sent to your Russian relative, Mr. Ivan Turnikov."

"What kind of hint? What are you talking about, detective?"

173

"I'm talking about the paintings stolen from the Russian Museum in St. Petersburg, Mr. Winder."

"I don't quite understand, detective. I am an American diplomat, and I don't have the slightest idea what you're talking about. I think we can stop our conversation at this point until I invite the consulate lawyer to join us."

"I don't think that it would be in your interest, sir," Jacob said carefully.

Then he took a tape recorder from his briefcase, put it on the table in front of the consul, and punched the play button. When the twenty-minute tape finished, a heavy silence hung in the room. Norman Winder didn't interrupt it. Big drops of sweat covered all his face. They fell to the desk, but he didn't wipe his face.

Jacob was the first who interrupted the silence.

"Mr. Winder, you are a clever man and understand that it would not be too smart to deny your participation in this crime. Your action, intentionally or not, has caused the death of two people, Mr. Ivan Turnikov's wife and his daughter, your daughter-in-law, Ana."

Norman Winder's self-assurance had vanished, and he hectically tried to analyze the situation that had totally had changed for him. But instead of cold analysis, only one thought lived in his mind: this is the end. His head pounded so that he had to press his temples with both hands. But it brought no ease. The vein in his temple pulsed: end, end, end…

"I didn't know that his wife was murdered," he whispered at last.

"You're dealing with the Russian Mafia, sir. It's far crueler than the Italian. They won't stop murdering until they receive the money. Who will be the next, your grandchildren?"

"I only sent the canvases by diplomatic mail. I didn't know they were stolen from the museum. Ivan Turnikov told me that a Russian private collector intended to sell the paintings at auction, but hadn't received a permission to go through customs."

"Not just that, sir," Jacob said coldly. "You've forgotten to return the pictures to the addressee, and that caused the death of two innocent people."

Norman Winder sighed deeply.

"I don't know what happened to me. I couldn't give them away. When I saw the pictures and thought that I held millions of dollars in my hands … I don't know what happened to me," he repeated bitterly. "It was beyond me. And now my life is ruined." In despair, he buried his head in his hands.

"Russia is interested in returning the pictures to the museum. As per my talks with Russian authorities, they would insist, through the Interpol, on your extradition and trial. They realize it would only be a formality. You have diplomatic immunity and, of course, will not be extradited. But if you cooperate and return the pictures, they would drop all charges against you. I can also offer you, Mr. Winder, total immunity against criminal charges at home. My boss had discussed this matter with the DA. It's a good deal, believe me. You'll finish your diplomatic career and resign honorably to start a new life." Jacob changed the tape in the tape recorder. "Can I switch it on, sir?"

Norman Winder sighed deeply and nodded. "Yes," he said hoarsely.

When his confession was recorded, he raised his eyes to Jacob.

"Will you do me a great favor, detective? Please, don't send your people to take the paintings out of the basement of my

Pennsylvania house. That is a prestigious neighborhood, and if the police arrive, I won't be able to live there." He inhaled deeply. "I'll deliver the pictures to the police headquarters myself."

"I will," Jacob promised, although he felt no pity for this man.

When Jacob left the American consulate, his thoughts were already far away from man's greed and stupidity.

29.

On Sunday, the next day after Shabbat, in the hour after sunset, Jacob dialed the number that Moses had given him.

"May I speak to Rabbi Korinetz, please?"

"Who is calling?" asked pleasant woman's voice.

"I am Jacob Reterseil, from New York."

"Hold on, sir."

"Papa, Mr. Jacob Reterseil from New York is on line. Do you expect his call?" Jacob heard in the receiver.

Then Jacob heard the man's voice, "Good evening, Mr. Reterseil. Rabbi Korinetz speaking."

"Good evening, sir. My father, Dr. Moses Reterseil, told me that you had kindly agreed to talk to me. I'm collecting some material for my future book," he explained briefly.

"It would be my pleasure to see Dr. Reterseil's son in my house." Rabbi's voice was pleasant and sounded young. "Tomorrow at four o'clock is okay for you?"

"It's a perfect time, sir."

"See you tomorrow, Jacob." Rabbi Korinetz hung up.

All that evening, Jacob tried to concentrate on the upcoming conversation with the rabbi, but the more he thought about it, the more his thoughts were mixed up. Finally he fell asleep, but his sleep was short. He opened his eyes and switched on the light on the night table. Jacob's glance stopped on the Bible that was part of every hotel room. A bookmark was inside the book. He opened it at *Proverbs*, and his eye caught the verses someone else had marked.

Because I have called and ye refused, I have stretched out My hand and no man regarded; I also will laugh at your calamity; I will mock when your fear cometh.

He had never thought of God laughing before – of God mocking. Jacob sighed. This God is a myth, and time would prove it. Why do we create myths? Do we need to put our sins on somebody's shoulders? Jacob was about to close the Bible, but before he did, another sentence attracted his eye.

"Now is the accepted time."– 2 Cor. Vi. 2.

Accepted time of what? The transfusion of souls? The Messiah's coming?

Like one who passes through a strange and wondrous experience, then slowly recalls every item of that experience, Jacob went mentally slowly over the story of Rabbi Lieberman's death. Then he switched the light off.

A myriad of thoughts crowded his brain. He gave up on the perplexing attempt to think out the problem, telling himself that the approaching new day would take care of itself. And with that thought, he fell asleep.

*

Waking up, Jacob was nervous. What will he talk about with the rabbi? What right did he have to interfere in the life of this man? Preoccupied, he had a light breakfast, and then, to kill time until four o'clock, he tried to concentrate on reading *Zohar*.

Evil and impurity are often referred to in the Zohar as "the other side" (sitra archra), meaning the side distinct from, and opposed to holiness. Evil is also referred to as 'kelipah'; literary shell or bark. The kelipah conceals within it a spark of holiness which is a vital force by virtue of which the 'kelipah' exists, analogous to a fruit surrounded by a shell or peel. In order to release the holy spark, the encumbering shell must be removed.

The Zohar distinguishes among four 'kelipot', three of which are entirely evil. The forth 'kelipat nogah' is the shell which actually envelops the spark of holiness.

But looking at the book, he was still thinking, reviewing all the circumstances of his peculiar situation.

*

Rabbi Korinetz' house was far from Jacob's hotel. Before hiring a cab, he decided to walk along the road to think over the upcoming conversation.

The street in front of the hotel was crowded with people demonstrating against killing animals. To escape the group that almost blocked the pavement, Jacob turned abruptly into the road and literally ran into the arms of a man.

"Jacob!"

"Bill!"

The greeting flew simultaneously from the lips of the two men. They shook hands.

"By all that's wonderful!" cried Bill, still wringing Jacob's hand. "Being in Australia and knowing you are in New York, I've just met you here as soon as I thought about you!"

"Thought about me?"

"Oh, let's get out of this crush, old chap," interrupted Bill.

Bill was a man of Jacob's age, already flabby, with horn glasses and a walrus moustache. He sparkled with energy. They had studied together at NYU Law School, and although they had never been friends, kept in touch with mutual sympathy. Jacob heard that after graduation, Bill had married an Australian woman and moved to Australia.

In the comparative lull of a walk, Bill went on.

"You know, Jacob, my father-in-law is the CEO of one of the biggest Australian corporations that controls a lot of Australia industry. I work for him as a corporate lawyer," he explained and looked at Jacob. "Maybe we can stop at a café?"

"Sorry, Bill, today I'm pressed for time," Jacob said.

"Okay, I'll explain everything to you on our way. Several weeks ago important papers were stolen from my father-in-law's safe; from his personal safe. I hadn't the slightest idea of the combination as the safe was in his house, not the office," Bill clarified.

Jacob looked at Bill questioningly, but didn't ask questions.

So Bill continued, "I don't know why, but he didn't call the police. He desperately needs his papers back and, as he told me, he's ready to pay any price for them."

"Why does he need them now?" Jacob asked matter-of-factly.

"I don't know…He was going to sell the main Canberra newspaper," Bill said thoughtfully.

"Do you have any idea, Bill, what kind of documents you are talking about?"

"I do have one clue." Bill looked at Jacob carefully. "His father Otto Schidler had started his Australian business with nothing, after the WWII. He had emigrated from Germany," Bill said and looked at Jacob from behind his glasses. "I suppose the missing papers concerned his Nazi past."

Jacob looked at his watch. "I've got a very important meeting soon, Bill."

"What about my offer? I thought that only you could find out who could be interested in those papers. He offers big money," Bill reminded.

"I'm afraid that's not my business, Bill. I am neither a private detective nor a Nazi hunter. I would speculate that your father-in-law's dad had a business partner who shared the same Nazi past. Maybe he was afraid that those documents would appear in the newspaper after the business was sold and the new owner wouldn't be controlled by your relative. But that's only my speculation, Bill. I think you shouldn't worry. If the man who stole papers needed money, he would already be in contact. If he were a guy, who intended to expose your father-in-law dad's Nazi past, he would already have published those documents. If nothing has happened in the weeks since the theft, it means your relative can sleep calmly."

"I'm sorry that you aren't interested in this job, Jacob," Bill said heartily. "But thank you for the advice. If you find, while you're staying in Australia, time for lunch with me, it would be wonderful to share recollections about our good, old times." Bill handed Jacob his business card and said emotionally again, "Our meeting was unbelievable! When I saw you, I thought that my mind had materialized you. Now I'm sure it really was the materialization of an idea. Unbelievable!"

When Jacob and Bill had finally parted, Jacob looked at his watch. There was barely time to hire a cab to go to Rabbi Korinetz' house. He flagged down a passing cab. The driver was a silent companion, and Jacob enjoyed the peace. But he couldn't concentrate on the upcoming visit; his head was empty. Thinking of his chance meeting with old fellow Bill, Jacob grinned. For the second time in a short period, he had rejected big money. Was he an altruist or an idiot? Money! Did it play a role in his life? Would it change his life if he had it? What nonsense comes to my mind, he thought, and at that moment the driver stopped the car in front of a big, two story brick house.

"Your destination, sir," the driver said, and Jacob thought that no driver in New York would say such pleasant words to a passenger.

Destination. Is Rabbi Korinetz' house his destination?

Jacob paid for the ride and went to the front door. He rang, and almost immediately the door opened to reveal a tall, beautiful young lady with that inquisitive coloring and smoothness of complexion that was the product of a natural, organic life. Her face couldn't be pronounced wholly beautiful, but it was a face that was full of life and charm.

Jacob bowed. "My name is Jacob Reterseil, miss."

"I know." She smiled. "I'm Judith. My dad is waiting for you, sir. Please, come in."

Jacob came and looked around. The room was a large

one, exquisitely furnished and filled with books. A small but cheerful, wood fire burned on a tiled hearth. A man rose briskly from a couch and the warm, mellow light that filled the room seemed to clothe him as he stood to meet Jacob.

"I'm glad you came, Mr. Reterseil," Rabbi Korinetz said as he gestured toward a chair. "May I call you Jacob?"

"Of course you can, sir," Jacob said. He looked openly at the rabbi. One glance at his face was sufficient to tell Jacob that Rabbi Korinetz was a warm-hearted, unconventional, not impulsive, reserved, clever man – a perfect rabbi in appearance, and a perfect gentleman in his manners.

"Darling, let me introduce Dr. Moses Reterseil's son," he said, turning to the very beautiful lady in her fifties, who was sitting on the couch. "I told you about him," he reminded. Then the rabbi added, addressing Jacob, "My wife Esther."

"I remember," she said and smiled warmly at Jacob. "Welcome to our house, Jacob."

"Esther," the rabbi told his wife. "I think Jacob won't refuse drinking a cup of tea with us."

"We'll take care of it, darling," she said, and both women went to the kitchen.

Jacob felt tension growing in him, but couldn't understand the source of that feeling. He felt like a student sitting in front of a teacher.

"Anyway, Jacob, Dr. Reterseil wrote me that you were going to write a book. What will this book be about?"

"I'd like to describe the history of Orthodox Judaism, sir; to be precise, the history of its different branches, and its spread over the world, including Australia."

"There are many books dedicated to that subject. In what aspect will your book be different from them?" Rabbi Korinetz asked.

Jacob sighed. He felt the coming conversation on that theme would not be easy for him.

"The main Orthodox flow is broken into many different streams. Major groups include the Satmar, Lubavicher, Bobover, Belzer and others. I'd like to show what their main differences are, and why today we cannot talk about Orthodox Judaism as a whole. In some aspects, these differences separate us Jews, instead of unifying us." Jacob said, feeling that continuing would put him in an awkward position.

"This is a big theological job, Jacob. It would be rather difficult to complete this noble mission without having a rabbinical education," Rabbi Korinetz said, and Jacob heard light irony in his words. "You see, Hassidism is less a movement of ideas of its own, but rather one in which the ideas found in classical Jewish sources, especially the *Kabbalah*, are given a new life and fresh emphasis. The task of discovering on what this emphasis consists is difficult because each of the early masters had his own interpretation of Hassidic doctrine. But if you, later on, formulate detailed questions for me, I'll try to give you detailed answers," Rabbi Korinetz offered.

"Thank you, sir, I'll think over the questions," Jacob said, feeling more and more uncomfortable.

Fortunately, Esther and Judith called them to the dining room where they had set the table for tea. Jacob sat opposite Judith, and every time he raised his eyes to hers, his tension grew.

Although he was charmed by her easy, unconventional manners, his mind was full of anticipating unexpected questions that Rabbi Korinetz might give him. But the rabbi did not ask any difficult queries.

"How is your father, Jacob?" Rabbi Korinetz asked.

"Since I have had correspondence with him, I realized that Dr. Reterseil is a great man, a dedicated man."

"Thank you, sir. He's all right. Although he has stopped practicing medicine, he is still a consultant at Maimonides Hospital in Brooklyn where he had worked for almost fifty years."

"I know Maimonides Hospital quite well," the rabbi said. "During one of my visits to the U.S., I became ill and was hospitalized there. But then I did not yet know your father." Rabbi Korinetz smiled. "And my daughter Judith worked there as a young intern."

Jacob raised a brow in surprise. Esther saw it and smiled.

"She's a doctor, Jacob. She is the head of pediatric services in our local hospital," Esther added, and Jacob saw that she was proud of her daughter.

"Frankly, Judith, when I saw a piano back in the sitting room, I had decided that you are a pianist," Jacob said, turning to her.

Judith laughed. "Don't be confused, Jacob. Mama is the pianist. She had graduated from Julliard."

"Anyway, you are a writer, Jacob?" Esther asked.

"Not really," Jacob said frankly. "It's what my father wants me to be, and now I feel the interest in this kind of activity. But by my education, I'm a lawyer; I graduated from the NYU Law School. I'm a corporate lawyer," he clarified.

"What was the main purpose of your visit to Australia?" Esther asked.

"My work," Jacob answered frankly. "A friend from my university, also a corporate layer, invited me here to discuss a sensitive matter," Jacob said. He thought that an accidental meeting with Bill was sent from Above to justify his visit here. "Sensitive documents were stolen from the safe of the corporation founder, a man who had a Nazi past," he explained. "I can speculate that the corporation was founded with money belonging to Jews killed in concentration camps. But what does that change now?" Jacob looked at Rabbi Korinetz's face.

"You're right, Jacob, nothing," the rabbi agreed, and Jacob felt that the rabbi was satisfied when he heard Jacob's tale. "If you remember, the Nazi hunter Symon Wiezenthal fiercely defended Nazi criminal Kurt Waldhaem while he was the United Nations Secretary-General. He called Kurt Waldhaem his friend, in spite of the fact that he knew of documents justifying Kurt Waldhaem's Nazi war crimes. Good and bad are too mixed up in our world. That's why we, Hassidim Jews, try to distance ourselves from the material world."

"Can Hassidim be beyond society, rabbi?" Jacob asked. He felt his tension gone and changed the topic of the conversation to one closer to the point of his interest.

"It's not easy, of course. My predecessors were from Russia, and I can't forget the words of the Russian Bolshevik leader Vladimir Lenin, 'living in society, nobody can be free of it.' The only way for us is to live beyond society," the rabbi said firmly. "With the help of the *Kabbalah*," he added. "Depending upon the *Kabbalah,* we can develop a rich, mystical tradition. A union with God can be reached through *ecstatic prayer* and the earnestly desired coming of the Messiah."

"The Satmar, the Bobov, the Telem, and, more visibly, the Lubavicher have hereditary, localized dynasties of the Rebbes. After Ba'al Shem's death, the Rebbes inevitably began to acquire more power. Can it create a new bitter disappointment for the Jews like the messianic career and apostasy of Sabbatai Zvi?" Jacob asked carefully.

Rabbi Korinetz peered at him from under his glasses.

"If you're going to reveal your doubts in your book, you definitely will be scolded." A tiny smile touched the rabbi's lips. "Many of Rebbe Menahem Mendel's followers hailed him as a messiah and went about singing in public places, 'we want the messiah now,' in the hope that God would reveal his true identity as the hoped-for-redeemer to the Rebbe, to the consternation of most of the other Hassidim and Orthodox rabbis. The latter were now slow to point out the danger of unbridled messianic fervor, especially when the Messiah is identified with a particular, known leader."

A telephone call interrupted their conversation. Rabbi Korinetz took up the receiver. After a minute, he hung up and turned to Jacob.

"Your father and my daughter treat the human body; while a rabbi – human souls. A sick man needs desperately to talk to me, and I cannot refuse him. Please, don't be in a hurry to leave. I think my wife and daughter are not the worst hostesses." The rabbi smiled, turning to them. "And I hope that we'll continue our conversation in the future. Since you have already found the way to my house, you will always be welcome," Rabbi Korinetz said.

His words were so warm and sincere that Jacob felt very uncomfortable. "It's so kind of you, sir," Jacob murmured. How could I look in the man's eyes while intending to destroy him? He thought. My Lord, forgive me, he whispered, looking at Rabbi Korinetz' back.

Esther left the room with her husband, leaving Judith alone with Jacob, who felt that strange tension again. She was a woman, a beautiful, attractive woman. Her physical grace and beauty, the fit of her dress, the perfect harmony of it – all this now struck him. And the most surprising thing was the fact that he felt like a teenager who was unable to open his mouth near Judith. The silence was already too long.

"Esther," Jacob said at last. "I thought how I could have not met you when you studied in New York?" He felt his face flame from the foolishness of the question.

She responded seriously. "The Orthodox community is too big; it's the whole world."

"One of the worlds," he corrected. "Maybe back at that time, I was in another world." He looked at Judith openly.

"Maybe."

When Esther returned the room, Jacob said to her, "Would it be impertinent, Mrs. Korinetz, if I asked you to play something?"

Esther laughed. "That's too formal, Jacob. Please call me Esther; and I'll willingly play for you."

All three returned to the sitting room. Esther sat at piano, and Judith stood nearby to help her turn the music pages.

With the first chords of music, a wave of strange feelings flooded Jacob. Looking at the classical profile of the biblical Judith standing in front of him, he suddenly thought of how happy he would be if this beautiful young lady were his wife. But he, obviously, was too old for such a beauty. Listening to the Chopin nocturne, Jacob felt that his heart was also full of music. But he was still afraid to confess to himself that it was the music of unexpected love that flooded his heart. He had never felt this way before; he had never experienced it with any of the women that he had met in his entire life. It was something different; something inspiring, giving a new impulse to his life, forcing him to discard the past and look to the future with the expectation of the miracle.

Jacob closed his eyes. Why had God sent him to meet this girl?

Why did God give him a rare chance to feel the splash of his soul?

The music filled all the space around him; it filled his soul, his heart, his body. Jacob dissolved in the music, and he knew that the music fulfilled Judith's soul as it fulfilled his. It was music for them, only for them.

When the melodious sounds stopped, Jacob shuddered and opened his eyes. The music stopped, but the harmony between two hearts was not broken because he could still hear the music of Judith's heart. Gradually, Jacob was back to the reality. It was a time to say good-bye, and he stood up.

"Thank you for your hospitality and an unforgettable evening," he said, trying to avoid looking in Judith's eyes.

"You are always welcome in our house," Esther said cordially.

"I'll show you out, Jacob," Judith said. Then she accompanied him to the front door.

On the threshold, Jacob turned to her. "Judith, what would you say if such an old man as I invited you to lunch before I depart for New York? Please, say yes."

"I don't know why I shouldn't," Judith said, trying to keep an indifferent tone, and flashed a quick glance of enquiry at him.

His tone and glance were full of meaning. Before his ardent gaze, her eyes dropped and her color heightened visibly. She silently gave him her beautiful hand, and he kissed it. When was the last time that he, a police detective, had kissed a woman's hand?

After the door closed behind him, Jacob felt as if his heart was that of a young man again. Instead of hiring a cab, he walked along the street.

"Is life worth living!" he cried inwardly, answering his

own question with rapturous words. "In this hour I know nothing else in the world that could be given me to make life more joyous!"

People passing him noticed his face, radiant with wondrous joy. It was rare to see peace in the faces of people occupying our great cities. It was rarer to see joy's gleam. Jacob allowed his glance to flash all around him, as he murmured, "I'm glad that I'm in Millburn. It's not dull, grim or sordid like New York. Who was it who wrote, 'After traveling, one comes back home and finds it the most wonderful place of them all'? All big cities are the same, but Millburn is the most beautiful of all because Judith lives here."

Jacob laughed low and gleefully at his own merry mood. He moved forward in a strange rapture of spirit. How wonderful the world is: the wonderful weather, the wonderful city, wonderful Judith. The Perfect World.

Suddenly he heard, "For the love of God, good sir, would you give me some change? Not for drugs. I need to go home."

Jacob turned abruptly toward the voice. The girl's face was haggard; her eyes were wells of indifference. They were the empty eyes of a drug addict. She lied when she mentioned the name of God.

He slipped his hand into his pocket and took out the first coin that came to his touch. It was a nickel, but he felt uncomfortable giving it to the girl. He took out his wallet, and dropped ten dollars into the outstretched palm.

"God bless you, sir," she said mockingly.

He passed on, but the incident moved him strangely. His mood plummeted. He has no right to think about Judith.

He came to destroy her life. He is a policeman. It's his fate, his karma. It's God's punishment for him.

But when Jacob reached his rooms, the gloomy thoughts caused by the accidental meeting in the street had left him.

30.

It was almost midnight when Jacob returned to his hotel room, but he didn't go to bed. His soul was disturbed. The impressions of meeting Rabbi Korinetz and his family had stirred a myriad of disquieting thoughts within him.

Jacob liked the rabbi, his wife and their daughter. Why had he gone to the rabbi's house? The rabbi told him clearly that an Orthodox Jew could be free from the society in which he lived and couldn't be judged by the rules of that society. Rabbi Korinetz lived in expectation of the Messiah's coming. To live in His expectation means to purify a man's soul in every moment of his existence.

If He came today, came now, what about me? Jacob wondered. Where would I come in?

He was quite unprepared for the Messiah's coming, and he knew it. Jacob shivered slightly at the thought of his lack of preparation: he has come to destroy the man in lieu of purification of his soul. Why, in such a case, was he awarded with meeting the man's daughter?

Jacob had no doubt that meeting Judith was God's present to him. What was he awarded for? Who was he to consider himself a weapon of punishment? Who gave him, a stranger from the material world, the right to come to the world of spirit and say, I'm superior?

Jacob hated himself because he could not change his nature; he had become too much a police officer. The idea of justice lived inside him; this feeling was independent from all his other feelings. To discard that idea, he had to change his nature, to return to the world of his people, the world that he had left an age ago when he was a silly youngster. Where did he pick up that stupid idea of self-confirmation? He had lost himself in the jungle of the lowest of fifth worlds, material world *ASIYAH* – the world of sins and crimes, the world of lacking souls. Long ago he had persuaded himself that he was above that world, but he was only a part of it.

Trying to find the answers to his questions, Jacob shut himself up alone with the manuscript that his father had given him. He opened it, and in a moment he was mesmerized; he could not take his glance away.

Secret mystical traditions came to be known as Kabbalah, from the Hebrew word "kabeil"- "receive," simplifying the transmission of the esoteric tradition that was received by the leaders of that generation from the leaders of the previous generation. This tradition was interpreted and expounded in both its theoretical and practical aspects (Kabbalah Lyumit or contemplating Kabbalah, and Kabbalah Ma'asit or practical Kabbalah).

Kabbalah Lyumit sets out to explain the process whereby the created realm came into finite, tangible existence through the will of the infinite Creator. Kabbalah Lyumit also analyses the nature of the relationship between the creation, as it proceeded toward fulfilling the purpose for which it was created, and the divine source from which it emerged. On a deeper level,

Kabbalah Lyumit explores the complex nature of the divine reality itself – in particular, the paradox of God's simultaneous transcendence and consequent inability of man to gasp Him at all, together with His immanence, active and reactive relationship with creation and humanity.

Jacob closed his eyes and thought that his father was a genius in trying to express what was concealed in the mysterious labyrinth of the *Kabbalah* in plain words. With the increasing interest, he continued reading.

An additional aspect of contemplative tradition is the use of various meditative techniques to ponder the divine, manifestation of divinity, and esoteric underpinnings of the material world. These include the contemplation of divine names, of Hebrew permutations and of the ways in which the sefirot (supernal divine forces) harmonize and interact. Some ancient forms of Kabalistic meditation produced a visionary experience of supernal "chambers" and the angelic beings who occupy them. This is known as Hechalot tradition.

The practical tradition of the Kabbalah involves techniques aimed specifically at altering material states of events – techniques such as the incantation of divine names or the inscription of such names or those of the angels upon amulets. On occasion, these methods have been used to fashion a golem (humanoid) or some other creature. However Kabbalah Ma'asit is meant to be employed by only the most saintly and responsible of individuals, and for no other purpose than the benefit of man or the implementation of God's plan of creation.

Suddenly Jacob realized what had happened to Moshe de Leon and what caused his unexplained death after he had promised to show the ancient manuscript of *Zohar* to his young companion Ben-Shmuel. When he found the technique to join Rashbi's soul, and Rashbi dictated *Zohar* to him, God justified it as a benefit for mankind. But the next time, when de Leon used the technique for his personal benefit, his attempt was rejected and he was punished with death.

There are some indications of these techniques being abused by unfit practitioners. The great Kabbalist Rabbi Luria himself admonished his disciples to avoid the art of practical Kabbalah as he deemed such practice unsafe. He considered the state of ritual purity that is necessary for the service in the Holy Temple remained unattainable.

In essence, however, there is no clear demarcation separating the contemplative elements of Kabbalah from those aimed at influencing or altering existence. Just as Kabbalah Iyunit, through its system of kavanot (guided meditations), can influence the configuration of divine forces, impinging upon our reality, so too is the efficacy of "practical Kabbalah" predicated upon the knowledge of Kabalistic theory and doctrine.

Kabbalah Iyunit has thus been characterized as a descriptive "anatomy" of divine reality. Kabbalah is concerned with the technical identities and "locations" of, and the relationship between, the worlds (planes of reality), the sefirot (divine emanations) and the order in which they evolve from one another and affect one another in the vast chain known in Kabbalah as the 'seder hishtalshelut.' Or the process by which divine energy (or "light") devolves from high spiritual planes to lower ones, eventually to become manifest in this physical plane of existence.

Of course, the ultimate intention of the Kabbalah is practical – to reveal the divinity manifested in the sefirot on each of the planes of reality rather than merely describe the emanations themselves. The ultimate intention of Kabbalah is to bring the individual, then the entire world – all plans of reality – into harmony with the Divine purpose for which they were initially created.

Jacob didn't notice how many hours he had spent reading. The night was almost gone when he looked up from his book. There was a wondering amazement in his eyes, as well as a strange perplexed knitting of his brows. It's all marvelous! He murmured, not feeling at all tired after his sleepless night. He felt like a curtain in front of his eyes had, at last, fallen.

Jacob smiled at himself as he rose to his feet. The sun had yet to show its face on the horizon when Jacob put on his coat and left the hotel. Ten minutes after leaving his room, he was in a small garden across the road.

Everything was eerily still and silent in the early morning hour. The calm suited his mood. He wanted to feel, as well as be, absolutely alone. There was a faint light from the invisible stars that stabbed the pearl gray sky. Jacob moved slowly, thoughtfully, through the paths of the empty garden.

A robin quietly flew across his path, perched upon a low piece of the iron fencing, glanced askance at him, and then darted to eat a morning meal peeping out of the damp sod. Two or three low, sleepy birds began their discordant quacking. The tremulous flute notes of a thrush made rich music in the morning air. The gray light of a dawning day moved into the horizon. The smell of the earth grew rank. The air grew keener. The east slow reddened. Slowly, thoughtfully Jacob turned back toward his hotel.

If the Messiah came at this instant, he wondered, how

many of us would be ready to meet Him? God help us! What blind fools we are!

As soon as Jacob was back, he put his *tefillin* on and read the morning prayer, Sh'ma. He read it longer than usual, and his soul trembled with love. Was his newly-born love for Judith a part of his love for God?

The prayer finally pushed the rest of his sleep away. Now all his thoughts were full of Esther. He remembered her every move, every smile, every silent eyebrow's lift during his talk to her father. The woman's image had never so filled his imagination. For many years Jacob considered himself a reserved man. He was wrong. Now all the emotions and feelings that had been compressed in his heart for many years were animated. Much to his surprise, Jacob had discovered that the world was full of emotions.

And he was a part of the world's emotions. For the first time in his life, he felt in total harmony with the surrounding world.

Jacob's mind trailed off to last evening's scenes. He saw Judith on the threshold of her house; every item of it started up. She was loveliness incarnated; her eyes were big, round and wide in their staring wonder at Jacob's appearance. He felt that there was a path of thunder in front of him. But it was a path not just for him; he felt the vibrations of Judith's soul.

31.

After the door closed behind Jacob, Judith stood motionless for an instant.

There is a moment in every woman's life when her heart warns her that a great event is coming in her life, when love is offered to her by the only man who ever would loom large enough in her consciousness to be able to affect her existence.

In the mirror she had caught a glimpse of herself and remembered the light of admiration she had read in Jacob's eyes when he opened the door and saw her for the first time.

The accidental meeting with that man, who came to talk to her father, had broken the tranquility of her soul. For years Judith was equally nice and indifferent to everyone around her – her colleagues at the hospital and her acquaintances in the synagogue she attended. She was a part of her family, and the family was her whole world. Her father-the sage, her talented mother, and several far from the reality family friends – that was her world for years; she had consciously restricted herself to the family's boundaries.

Judith's parents were too delicate to ask why such a pretty and clever girl paid no attention to any other men, most of who would be happy marry her. Only she knew why she did it.

Judith shook her head and returned to her room where her mother was sitting on the couch.

"He is a treat, Jacob I mean, with such a strange last name, Reterseil. What do you think, Judy?" she asked her daughter. Her lips smiled but her eyes were serious.

"He's a very nice person," Judith agreed.

"The first impression is always right, dear," Mother said with a smile in her eyes.

After talking for a short time, Judith rose. "Sorry, Mama, I'm tired," she said. "Tomorrow I'll have a difficult day at the hospital. Good night." She kissed her mom on the cheek and went to her bedroom.

As she lay across her bed with closed eyes, she couldn't sleep, being engrossed in recollections.

...There had been a donation party at the house of the U.S. Representative Zeev Hoffman, who had asked Judith's father to attend it with his family. By that time Judith was a senior at NYU Medical School. Now that party came back to her.

Things had been a bit stiff and formal at first as they often were at such gatherings. The people sat around and talked about current political topics, and how much kosher turkey would fetch for the Thanksgiving Day, whether it would pay best to buy them plucked or still feathered.

Then, for half an hour, her mother was the life of the party as she had performed a Chopin's composition. When she finished playing, everybody applauded enthusiastically.

Then all of the guests swam into another room to discuss the most sensitive topic – the amount of their donations.

As that matter did not interest her, Judith remained in her chair, still under the impression of Chopin's music. Suddenly she heard a voice behind her.

"Judy, are you going to supper with the first batch or will you wait for the next turn?" There was no self-irony in the man's tone; his tone was serious.

Turning, she found herself face to face with young Rabbi Shlomo, the host's son. His gaze was very warm, very ardent. Judith knew Shlomo had fallen in love to her, but her attitude toward him was only that of a friend. She did not see him as the man of her dreams.

She had railed him about his extra seriousness, but Shlomo had answered, "Don't, Judy. You must know why I'm grave and sad today."

"No, I don't," she had replied.

"I heard you're leaving New York for Australia in the very near future."

Judith had gazed at him in honest wonder, not fully grasping his meaning.

"Why should that make you sad, Shlomo?" she asked.

Shlomo had leaned closer towards her. There was no one to see them. Where her hand had rested on the arm of the chair, his large hand had moved, and her white fingers were clasped in his. His eyes had sought hers, and under the hypnotic power of the strong love in his eyes, she had been compelled to meet his gaze.

"I loved you, Judy. God only knows how I love you! It's beyond me." He exhaled noisily.

His clasp on her fingers had tightened and he had leaned nearer to her face. No man except her father had ever been so close to her before. Judith felt the warmth of Shlomo's breath, the heat of his flesh.

"I like you, Shlomo," Judith said, trying to release her hand, "but I cannot say I love you. I just don't feel it. You're a friend."

Luckily for her, at that instant there had come a rush of feet and the sound of many voices. Shlomo succeeded quickly in regaining his old unseen nook.

Except for one moment when she was leaving for home and Shlomo had helped her with her coat, he hadn't spoken directly to her again that evening. He had managed then to whisper, "God bless you, darling. Pray for me."

Soon after, Judith had graduated from NYU Medical School and they had moved to Australia where her father became the head of a small, but independent community of Orthodox Jews.

A piercing pain came to her when almost a year later, she heard that Rabbi Shlomo had committed suicide. It was a very rare case that an Orthodox Jew took his own life in contradiction of God's will.

Judith cried inconsolably. She asked herself repeatedly whether she could have saved Shlomo's life if she had said "yes" that evening. Her guilt was because she deprived him of hope. A man cannot live without hope. If she could have returned to the past, she would. Why hadn't she said that she wasn't ready to give him an answer then! Why hadn't she said that she had to check her feelings? But she hadn't said anything, and since then she was doomed to carry her guilt and pray for God's forgiveness. Was that her guilt?

It was all this that had risen so strangely in Judith's mind. Her eyes were full of tears. For a second she compared two lives – the wife of a young American rabbi with endless possibilities of doing good, and that of the wife of a divorced Jewish writer who was vane and eager to be popular.

Judith laughed through her tears and was a little amused as she told herself, "Oh, Jacob hasn't yet asked me to marry him. And, perhaps, he never would."

Still full of tears, Judith fell asleep at last, murmuring a prayer.

32.

A feeling of strange harmony flooded Jacob. With everybody. With everything. With people. With the world. He knew the reason for that harmony. He knew the name of that harmony. Judith. He repeated her name as a mantra. It sounded like music; all music of the world. Judith!

Jacob knew that meeting her had changed his life. He had become a new man. And that new man could not wait another day to see her. She had promised to meet him for lunch. So he had called her.

"Judy, this is Jacob," he said and heard the vibration of his voice.

"I'm glad you called me, Jacob," she said sincerely.

"You had promised to find time for lunch with me. I have to return home within two days," he said.

"I have another idea for today, Jacob. I want to invite you to my synagogue for a special service."

"What's special?"

"One can live an entire life time as a Jew and never see the ceremony that's about to take place today. It's what is known as 'Chalitza.' Have you heard of it, Jacob?"

"Frankly, I haven't. Will your father perform the ceremony?"

"No, he doesn't perform any services. I am going to attend with one of my colleagues and her brother. Will you join us? It's not too far from my home."

"Willingly, Judith," he said with excitement, and then wrote down the address she gave him.

*

When Jacob arrived at the synagogue door, he met Judith and her friends – a tall man in traditional Orthodox clothes, and a mousy looking short, plump woman of indifferent age. The man's eyes expressed a brief surprise when he saw that Jacob wore only a *kipa* on his head, indicating that he did not belong to the Orthodox community. They exchanged formal greetings, and Judith introduced Jacob as "an old friend of mine."

Then the party had separated; the two women going one way, to the female part of the synagogue, and the men – to another. The synagogue was filling very fast; presently it was packed to suffocation.

Jacob always liked a synagogue's atmosphere although he wasn't a frequent guest of his own. He liked seeing the hat-wearing men and the bewigged women, the gorgeous female finery.

As they occupied their seats, Jacob's new acquaintance, Elisha, had already opened the prayer book and was silently concentrating on it. Jacob felt that the man did not like him, but accepted him 'as is' because of Judith's introduction. If he was not married, Jacob thought, he was, definitely, falling in love to her.

Jacob also opened his book, but instead of reading a prayer, he raised his eyes to the second floor, trying to find Judith's face among all the other women. For an instant it seemed that he had succeeded, but at that moment the rabbi began to intone the opening words of the service, reading from the roll lying in front of him.

"If brethren dwell together, and one of them die and have no child, the wife of the dead shall not marry unto a stranger; her husband's brother shall take her to wife and perform the duty of the husband's brother to her... And if the man desires not to take his brother's wife, then let his brother's wife go to the gate unto the elders and say, 'My husband's brother refuseth to raise up his brother unto the name of Israel, he will not perform the duty of my husband's brother.'

Then the elder of the city shall call the man and speak unto him, and if he stands to it, and say, 'I do not want to take her;'

Then shall his brother's wife come unto him in the presence of the elder and loose his shoe from his foot, and shall spit in his face and shall answer and say, 'So shall it be done unto that man who will not build us his brother's house.'

And this name shall be called in Israel, 'the house of him that hath his shoe loosed.'"

Jacob followed every item of the service with close attention, but hadn't yet caught why Judith had invited him to attend this particular service.

Presently the parties especially concerned mounted the platform, which was backed with a huge square frame covered with a black cloth. This symbolized mourning for the dead husband. Three tall candlesticks held lit candles, their flames appearing weird and sickly in the daylight.

The rabbi stooped before the brother-in-law and took off the man's right shoe and sock. Another official washed the bare foot, wiped it with a towel, and cut the toenails.

A soft, white shoe was made especially for that occasion. The rabbi put it on the man's foot. The laces were very tightly twisted round the ankle and knotted securely.

Then there followed a seemingly interminable string of questions, put by the rabbi and answered by the brother-in-law. The catechism culminated in a few main questions.

"Do you wish to marry this woman?"

"I do not," replied the brother-in-law.

"For what reason?"

"I'm already married. My wife is living, and the law of the land that we live in does not permit my having more than one wife."

The reply rang clear and strong in the silent hall of the synagogue; the hush seemed to deepen as the rabbi asked, "Will you give this woman Chalitza?"

"Certainly, I will if she wishes it," replied the brother-in-law.

"Do you wish to receive Chalitza?" the rabbi asked, turning to the woman.

Jacob saw how the light of a great eagerness leapt into the beautiful woman's eyes. Her face glowed with the warmth of a sudden color as she replied, "I do wish for Chalitza, for I desire to marry again."

The rabbi's assistant gave her proper instructions, and she knelt before her brother-in-law. With the thumb and finger of her right hand – she dare not use her left – she began untying the knots in the laces around the man's ankle.

It was not child's play. The knots had been drawn very tight; but she was very determined. Presently a deep sigh of relief broke from the breathless, watching congregation as she took the shoe from the man's foot. She flung it sharply down twice upon the floor.

The woman rose now to her feet to complete the ceremony. The law of spitting in the man's face had been modified to meet the view of a day less gross than then when it was carried out in full coarseness.

The brother-in-law took a couple of paces backward, and the beautiful widow spat on the place where he had stood a moment before. Then she faced the congregation. Her eyes traveled straight to the face of the man that she loved, a man she shortly was to marry. Her eyes danced with excitement, her cheeks were red with color, and her whole face was full of indescribable rapture.

"I'm free!" she cried.

"True, sister, you are free!" the brother-in-law responded.

The rabbi moved swiftly to her side and, looking into her face, said, "O, woman of Israel, you are free!"

The excited, perspiring congregation cried, "Woman, you are free!"

The service concluded a moment or two later, and the synagogue emptied.

Jacob's new acquaintance, Elisha, was still under the impression of the service. He turned to Jacob.

"Only the most Orthodox of Jews would dream of using Chalitza service to become free for re-marrying. This is the only case I personally know of," he said emotionally

"Yes, that was an extraordinary service," Jacob agreed.

At that moment Judith and her friend-woman joined both men.

"We were talking about this extraordinary service," Jacob

said, addressing Judith. "But I wonder what would have happened if she had failed to untie the shoe lace?"

"I had read of only one case that was held in the middle of the 18th century," Elisha said. "The widow failed to untie the lace and was disqualified to marry again."

After Judith's acquaintances stepped aside to speak to some friends, they walked along the street in silence. Jacob felt that Judith was under deep impression of the service, but he still couldn't understand why this service was so essential to her. The silence became too long. To break it, Jacob said again, "Thank you for bringing me to such an incredible service, Judith."

"It was!" Judith glanced away from him, but saw Jacob's eyes were full of the warmest admiration.

"Do you think, Judith, that if you were situated similarly to that beautiful woman, who we just saw freed from a Mosaic bond, that you would have braved the Chalitza ceremony or would you have taken advantage of English law?" Jacob asked.

Judith lifted her great, lustrous eyes to his in a sudden gaze of utter frankness.

"I would certainly not marry any man, who I could not wholly revere and love," she said, interrupting him.

"Happy the man who you would do this honor to, Judith!" Jacob said inwardly.

He barely whispered the words, and Judith was not wholly sure that he meant them for her ears. She didn't respond in any way. But she was conscious that his gaze was fixed upon her. She was equally conscious that she was blushing furiously. Perhaps it was to give her a chance of recovering herself that his next question was on quite a different topic.

"Would it be impertinent, Judy, to remind that you had promised me lunch together?"

"Unfortunately today I must work the afternoon shift at the hospital. But tomorrow I'm free. Tomorrow it would be my pleasure, Jacob," she said.

They had reached her house by this time.

"My best regards to your parents," Jacob said.

"I will." Judith handed him her hand. He pressed her fingers, and his eyes held an ardency that gave a new tumult to her heart.

Then Judith quickly opened the door and went inside.

33.

The last day of his stay in Australia approached, and Jacob's mood plummeted. Suddenly he realized that meeting Judith had changed his life forever. He came here to be a destroyer, but it was he who was destroyed. The police detective who had lived inside him for the last twenty years had died. His pursuit for the illusive self-confirmation now seemed him ridiculous; his intentions – laughable.

Shaving, Jacob looked in the mirror in the bathroom, but he didn't recognize his face. He had gotten accustomed of seeing self-assurance in his eyes; now his eyes reflected only confusion. He didn't like himself. For forty years he had played a role that was not written for him. He pretended to be a husband, a lover, a police officer. He pretended to be a Jew, although he had stopped being a Jew long ago.

He considered his life to be defined forever. Now he wasn't sure about tomorrow and was afraid of losing today. Today he was happy. He had a dream called Judith. Today he was happy because today he felt that it was still possible for him to find his way back to God.

All paths that lead to God are difficult, Jacob thought,

still looking at his reflection in the mirror. If they were not so far separated from God, He could get them in a moment's notice. We can anyway, if we could recognize that all our life, knowledge, freedom is within ourselves. Everything belongs to God, and we should therefore recognize the fact that it does.

Jacob finished shaving, washed his face, and then went to the chamber's window overlooking a quiet, narrow street. The working day had just begun; a new day, with new problems, new sorrows, and new joys. You cannot enter twice the same river; you also cannot remain the same man the next day, he thought.

Still preoccupied, Jacob sat on the couch. What had made him change? Did a couple of manuscripts written by his father allow him to touch the Torah's mysteries? Or had God changed him as if He had read Jacob's inner willingness to be changed?

He hadn't touched any mysteries. He could not touch them as the study of *Kabbalah* was restricted to a select few, qualified individuals. Maybe his father and Rabbi Korinetz were among those people; he was not. What he had realized was the fact that studying the esoteric dimension of the Torah was an obligation for the Orthodox Jew because it would be the catalyst to hasten the arrival of the Messianic redemption. He, a stray Jew, had only come to the threshold of the mystery; but even approaching it had changed his life.

Every Jew who came into this world carried his own special mission. Now Jacob understood that his mission in life was not to be a police detective. The past forty years had only been a preparation for fulfilling his mission. He had received the necessary experience to start the new life that God had given him. Would it be the life of a writer? What could he say to Jewish people to make them better and help them purify their souls? If he could do that, it would be a noble occupation.

"To make people better," Jacob repeated loudly. Who, but God, can make people better? No, he was wrong. God gave people the right to choose, but the direction in which they go depends on many factors, including who are their mentors. Was he ready to call himself a mentor? No. Mentors were people like his father and Rabbi Korinetz. He, Jacob, could only share his own experiences, his own mistakes and its corrections. He could anticipate that people would be able to avoid his mistakes. It would be his contribution to the mentors' work; in such a case he'd be able to call himself a mentor's helper. That is his vocation – to be a helper. Maybe all of us are the helpers of the great mentor – God? Jacob suddenly thought.

He could hardly wait until lunchtime.

When at last he had met Judith in the street, he realized that living in the moment was everything; a moment of happiness lasts an eternity.

"You are so beautiful, Judy!" he exclaimed.

She flushed. "Thank you, Jacob, for your kind words."

"I was afraid that today you would have an emergency at work, and I wouldn't see you before I go home. I'm so happy that you've come," he said sincerely.

They walked along the street.

"Where are we going?" Judith asked.

Jacob pointed in the direction of a sign in front of them, "Chinese Restaurant. Glatt Kosher." Beneath the sign there was a Star of David painted in an Oriental style. "It's the only kosher restaurant in this area," he said in apology.

Judith laughed. "You've made a good choice, Jacob. It's a very popular place, and usually it's always packed. If you didn't make a reservation beforehand, I'm afraid we'll have to stand in line."

Judith was right. When they arrived, the restaurant was full. But they were lucky; two customers had just cancelled their reservation. As Jacob and Judith were seated, the waitress, a young Chinese girl, came to their table to take the order. Jacob noticed the Star of David pendant on her chest.

After the waitress took the orders and stepped aside, he said, "I've read somewhere that in China there are only about three hundred Jewish families."

Judith smiled. "Her name is Rebecca. She has passed *giur* and married a Jewish man. She attends the same synagogue that I do," Judith explained. "There are more than a hundred Oriental women who have converted to Judaism in our town."

They ate an appetizer in silence, submerged in their own thoughts. Judith avoided Jacob's glance. But the silence became awkward, and she said, "Tell me about you, Jacob."

Jacob smiled. "Not too much to tell. I'm over forty. I was married, but am divorced now. No kids. All my life is my work. It was my work," he corrected himself. "What about you, Judith?"

Judith smiled sadly. "I think my life is even simpler than yours. I was born, then lived to study medicine when I was young. And now, that I'm a doctor, I live for my work. I'm thirty-four," she added.

"That's pretty young for such an old chick as me." Jacob grinned. Then he became serious. "Judith, I thank God for our meeting; but it also had made me unhappy; tomorrow I have to fly back to New York."

"I was also happy to meet you, Jacob. I felt as if I had known you for a long time," Judith said quietly. She held her breath in a strange ecstasy.

At that moment the waitress came to the table and asked for permission to seat two people at their table, as it was a four top table.

"Of course," Jacob agreed.

As another couple joined them, the frank conversation stopped. They finished their kosher Chinese meal quickly, and left the restaurant.

They walked along the street silently. Jacob held Judith's hand and felt like a youngster who walked with a girl for the first time in his life. Having seen a small garden, Jacob and Judith sat on a bench under a tree.

"Judith," he began as they sat. His voice was hoarse and deep.

She realized the meaning of the hoarseness. She knew by her own feelings that the depth and intensity of Jacob's voice was due to the emotion that filled him.

"Judith!" he repeated as a mantra, "I love you," he went on. "I have loved you from the first instant I met you. Maybe you think it's ridiculous to talk about love on the day after we met, but it's true. I know I would never pluck up the courage to tell you about it if I weren't flying home tomorrow. Please, don't tell me 'no'; don't tell me anything now. I only wanted you to know that I love you."

Judith knew that she would have found herself speechless at that moment had she tried to speak. But she did try; her lips moved, but no sound came out. She looked deeply into Jacob's eyes, and he read the answer.

With a sweeping gesture of passionate love, he gathered her up and showered kisses upon her cheeks. She lay like a stunned thing in his arms. Her joy was almost greater than she could bear.

Then as his hot lips sought hers, she awoke from her semi-trance of ecstasy and with a little sob she flung her arms upwards.

"I love you too, Jacob," she whispered. "Only God knows how much I love you! I know I don't need to tell you with these words." Her voice was stifled with a little rush of tears.

"And will you marry me?" Jacob's gaze burnt into her eyes, asking for an answer.

Judith wasn't able to reply for a moment. Her heart beat with a tumultuous gladness when she whispered, "I will."

There was an intensity of a mighty love in her utterance of those two words.

Time stopped for both of them.

"I'll leave you just for a short time, Judy, "Jacob said at last, interrupting the silence. "I'll be back to ask your parents' blessing."

"I'll wait," Judith whispered. Her eyes were full of tears of happiness.

34.

The American Airlines plane landed at the JFK airport at two o'clock afternoon. It was Friday, and Jacob decided not to show his face at police headquarters until Monday morning. Before he hired a taxi, Jacob called Moses.

"Hi, dad. I'm back and will see you on Shabbat," Jacob said when he heard his father's voice.

"It sounds great, son. Hearing your voice, I think you're in good spirits."

"I'm always in good spirits when I return home." Jacob felt he was smiling. He still felt the warmth of Judith's lips.

He was tired as he hadn't slept a moment in the plane, so after he took shower, he lay on the couch to take a nap. But he was too weary to sleep. The longer he lay there, the more Judith occupied his mind. He opened his eyes and only then noticed the flashing light on the answering machine. He stood up and pressed the button.

"Hi, Jacob. This is Sarah. I haven't heard from you for a long time. I hope you're okay. When you have a chance, give me a call."

Sarah! Jacob knew that Sarah loved him and, in the depth

of her soul, dreamed that one day their friendship would transfer into love. Now he had to bring her pain. What could he say? 'Hi, Sarah. By the way, I fell in love with someone and am going to marry her.' The memory of his passing fancy with Sarah had crossed his mind.

I liked her, admired her, he mused. I enjoyed her frank, open friendship, but love her – no. That word cannot be named in the same breath as my feeling for Judith. Jacob decided to postpone his conversation with Sarah; he was not ready for it.

His thoughts again returned to Judith. He suddenly realized that he wasn't quite frank with her. He didn't tell her the truth about his life, his job, his friendship with Sarah. Maybe knowing the truth about the aim of his meeting with her father, would she change her mind about marrying him?

Jacob went to the desk. He put in front of him a blank sheet of paper. For an instant Jacob was motionless. Then his pen flew over the surface of the paper. But his thoughts were even quicker than the pen. His whole being was palpitated with love. It was the love of his highest ideal. The love that he had sometimes dared to hope for might some day would be his, love that he had scarcely dared to expect. He tried to confess his sins, but confessed his love instead, pouring out all the wealth of emotion of his heart to his beautiful betrothed. When he had finally finished his confession, he put the paper in an envelope and sealed it quickly, not reading the text again as he was afraid that his bravery could volatilize. How senseless of me not to have told Judith everything, he muttered.

Jacob smiled a little to himself as he murmured, "May I take this bit of negligence as a sign that divine love is predominant with me rather than human? Or was it that I wasn't sufficiently instructed about human love in the school?"

*

Despite Jacob's lack of rest after the flight, he felt fresh when he entered his father's house just before sunset.

"I'm glad to be home, dad," he said, kissing Moses on the cheek and embracing Berta.

After the candles were lit and the short Shabbat prayer spoken, Moses asked, "Did you meet Rabbi Korinetz?"

"I did. He's a great man."

"And…"

"I realized how stupid I was, dad."

"Stupidity is a treatable disease, son." Moses smiled. "I see your happy face, Jacob. Does that mean you have recovered?"

"It does, with your help, dad. I've re-evaluated my life and understood that it's not too late to start a new one," Jacob said, with the smile of someone who had achieved his goal.

Moses looked at his son attentively.

"Do you think your new life will be different from the old one?"

"Positively, dad. I'll start with my work; I'm going to resign."

"Are you? Why?" Moses' surprise was sincere.

"After meeting Rabbi Korinetz, I've realized that people's justice often contradicts God's," Jacob said thoughtfully.

"What are you going to do after you resign, son?"

"You wanted me to become a writer." Jacob smiled. "I'll

try to fulfill your wish. Seriously, I will. I won't be able to write about religious concepts; definitely not. I'd like to become a fiction writer."

"Fiction? What could you write about?"

"I'll try to write a novel based on my own life," Jacob said thoughtfully. "If God gives me inspiration," he added.

"I'll pray for it, son."

"And I dream to live until the day, Jacob, that I read your novel," Berta said as she came in from the kitchen with a freshly made strudel. "Taste it, my boy; it's done especially for you," she muttered.

For some minutes they kept silent, testing the strudel. Then Jacob said, "Dad, I want to start my new life not alone. I'm going to marry, and I want to receive your blessing."

Happiness sparkled in Moses' eyes. Then he said, "You know how I love her, Jacob."

"Sarah would be a great wife for you," Bertha agreed.

"I'm not going to marry Sarah, dad." Jacob sighed heavily.

Suffering reflected in Moses' eyes, but he said nothing. He has found another *shiksa*, Moses thought. This thought was so painful that he pressed his right temple with his fingers to minimize the unexpected headache. The room was very still, awesomely silent. Moses closed his eyes.

"I'm going to marry Rabbi Korinetz' daughter." Jacob swallowed.

Moses heard Jacob's words, but not trusting what he had heard, he rolled his eyes.

"Rabbi Korinetz's daughter?" he asked.

"I love her, dad. And she has agreed to become my wife."

"In just a few days after you had met each other?" Bertha surprised, trying to settle herself more comfortably in a chair.

"My Lord," she whispered, "you have heard my prayers." Her emotions almost choked her.

"It's from God, Bertha. Either He gives love or not. What does time mean in love?" Jacob asked as he asked the question to himself.

"What does time mean in love?" Moses repeated the question. "Nothing," he agreed. Then, addressing the woman, he said, "Bertha, please bring us a bottle of Manischewitz. Today is the happiest day of my life!"

When Bertha brought a new bottle from the kitchen, Moses opened it and poured wine into the glasses.

"To your happiness, son," he proposed. "Thanks to God, will be blessed His name."

After they drank, Jacob said, "You know, dad, I still have one unanswered question."

Moses looked at him carefully.

"Why had been the letter *alef* that I saw on Rabbi Lieberman's chest? He was a *tzaddik*, and it would be expected to see the letter *tzaddi*. "

"I also wondered about that," Moses said thoughtfully. Then he stood up, went to a nearby shelf, and picked up a book. He opened it and read,

"The Holy One, blessed be He, created the world and all created beings through the Torah. Regarding the Torah, the verse states, 'God made me (the Torah) as the beginning of His way, the most primal of his works from the outset of time.' (Mishlei 8:22)"

Moses closed the book and continued, "Rabbi Hamnona Sabba explained that when it arose in the Will of the Holy One, blessed be He, to create the world, all the letters of the

Hebrew alphabet were concealed. For two thousand years prior to the actual creation of the world, the Holy One, blessed be He, gazed upon the letters and delighted in them. Then, when he chose to actually create the world, all the letters came before him in reverse order, from *tav* to <u>alef.</u>"

"But why was the letter *alef* chosen to appear on Rabbi Lieberman's body?" Jacob asked again. He hasn't yet caught what his father was talking about.

"I tried to make sense of it, Jacob. *Alef* is the first letter of the Hebrew alphabet, but God didn't choose it to create the world. So, it's not the letter of the beginning." Moses said thoughtfully.

"But it doesn't symbolize the end either."

"You told me that you saw the already vanishing letter *alef,* didn't you?"

"That's right," Jacob said. He hadn't yet understood Moses' point.

"When you saw the letter *alef,* Jacob, it was the last vanishing letter of the word written on the Rabbi Lieberman's chest."

"What do you mean, dad?" Jacob raised his brow in surprise.

"The rest letters written on Rabbi Lieberman's body had already vanished when you came in," Moses explained. "They were letters *heh, mem,* and *shin.* The combination of *alef, shin, mem, and heh* – that was written on Rabbi Lieberman's chest."

"*The guilt?*" Jacob couldn't express his surprise as the sense of translation of this Hebrew word into English has come to his mind.

"Yes, the guilt," Moses verified.

"What guilt?"

"God knows," Moses whispered.

"Does it mean the attempt of soul transfusion was sinful?" Jacob asked.

"I don't think so," Moses said quietly. "If the Torah opens such an opportunity, it means it can be done."

"But what could 'guilt' mean?" Jacob insisted.

Moses sighed. "God knows," he repeated. Then he poured more wine in their glasses. "Let's drink to happiness, son. Today I have realized that happiness is the absence of unhappiness. My unhappiness was created by the feeling of disharmony between my own soul and the soul of the world. Now my disharmony has vanished, and I can say that life is beautiful. I'm grateful to God for my happiness. I'm a happy man, son."

35.

Monday morning the rain was heavy. Jacob forgot his umbrella, and running into headquarters, he got drenched to the skin.

"You look like a wet chicken," Captain O'Burke said instead of his normal greeting when he saw Jack.

"I do," Jacob agreed, gingerly lowering himself in the chair near the captain's desk.

"I know the results of your trip to Australia," the captain said. "Norman Winder returned the stolen pictures, and we have already sent them to the Russian General Consulate. After that, the consul called the mayor to thank everyone who helped in return the paintings to the Russian Museum. You are the hero of the day, Jack," Captain O'Burke said, a little ironically as usual. Then he discarded the irony. "A new case is waiting for you, Jack. And, as always, it's urgent." He took out a green folder out of his desk drawer and thrust it toward Jacob.

But Jacob didn't take it.

"I'm going to refuse this one, captain," he said firmly.

Then, answering O'Burke's surprised look, Jacob handed the captain a piece of paper that he extracted from his pocket.

O'Burke scanned it, then his eyes widened.

"Are you kidding me, Jack?'

"No, I'm serious, captain."

"Why?" O'Burke asked. "If you are not satisfied with your salary, I can promise to increase it significantly. I have already sent my recommendation to the commissioner that you be appointed to the new position of Senior Principal Detective, one created especially for you."

"It's not a matter of money, captain."

"You don't like me as your boss or you don't like my attitude?"

"Captain, it has been my pleasure to work with you; you're a good man." Jacob laughed. "Maybe even better than you think you are."

"But, then, why?"

"I am a Jew," Jacob said thoughtfully. "Maybe it's a matter of self-respect."

"You are the most respected Jew in headquarters."

"I'm going to get married, captain," Jacob said as it could explain his intention.

"I congratulate you, Jack, with all my heart, and hope you won't forget to invite me to your wedding ceremony. But I don't understand how your marriage will affect your job."

"She is an Orthodox Jewish woman, captain. To marry her I have to go back to my people and become Jewish again."

"You've never stopped being a Jew, Jack. You wear your *kipa* on your head; it tells everybody who you are."

Jacob laughed. "How many Christian people wear a cross on their chest, but do not trust in God? I wear *a kipa*, but I distanced myself from God. I have to get back to my people," Jacob repeated. "This is the only reason for my resignation. Please understand me, captain; my decision to resign is firm."

Silence came. Captain O'Burke looked at the man sitting in front of him.

"I won't sign your resignation now, Jack. Please take another ten days to think over your decision," he said. "I do hope you'll change your mind. Don't be stupid, Jack. Although you have twenty years in service, you will not be able to collect social security until you are sixty-two. Your pension tier gives you a chance to collect the pension at fifty after twenty-five years in service. How can you give up your pension?"

As Jacob didn't answer the question, O'Burke continued his monologue, "If you decided that your job contradicts your religion, modify your work, Jack. If you don't want to wear a gun, don't. If you want to wear the full orthodox outfit, do it. I think the commissioner will issue special permission for you, taking into account your contributions to the department. If you do not want to work in the field, don't; I'll change your title from detective to senior management consultant. What you have to do Jack is only to generate ideas." Then Captain O'Burke threw in his last argument. "If you're married, Jack, you have to take care of your family. You haven't taken any bribes, so you have to work to support your family. Don't be too far from the reality." At last he stopped talking and extended his hand to Jacob. After Jacob shook it and stood up, O'Burke said, "I will not sign your resignation, Jack. Your work is your vocation. If you have found your way to the police, it's from God. Everything is from God, Jack. Don't forget it."

Jacob sighed. "Everything," he agreed, heading to the door.

The Jew is incredible, Captain O'Burke told himself again, looking at Jacob's back as he closed the door behind him.

Jacob returned to his office and, until lunch, took care of his paperwork. The rumors about his upcoming resignation had already spread over the department, and some of his fellow-detectives came to him to express how sorry they were to hear the news.

Amid all these polite conversations, he firmly decided to talk to Sarah. He called her but couldn't reach her. He left a message on her answering machine. He knew it was a very dry message.

"Sarah, my friend, I was too busy with my work to even give you a call. There have been big changes in my life. I fell in love with Rabbi Korinetz' daughter; I'm going to marry her. Soon I'll fly back to Australia, but while I'm home, I do hope to see you. You were and you are my best friend, Sarah. Kiss you."

Only when Jacob stopped talking did he hear a short buzz; his message was too long. But he didn't know at what place his message was cut off. He thought it was worth repeating, but he couldn't do it.

Jacob sighed. They say that friendship is a higher feeling than love, he thought. Maybe that's the point of view of people who hadn't experienced true love?

36.

Not without hesitation, Jacob called Australia. He was afraid that Judith would pick up the receiver and that could put both of them in an awkward position. But luckily, he didn't hear Judith's voice.

"Hello."

"Mrs. Korinetz? This is Jacob Reterseil from New York. Do you remember me?"

"Jacob, you are not a man to be forgotten the next day after meeting you. Do you want to talk to my husband?"

"If it's convenient."

"It is. Hold on, please."

Jacob heard Rabbi Korinetz ask his wife who it was. Then he heard the calm rabbi's voice in the receiver, "Rabbi Korinetz's listening."

"This is Jacob Reterseil from New York, sir. Would it be impertinent to ask whether you have time to see me again? It's very important for me, sir," Jacob added.

"When are you flying to Australia, Jacob?"

"In a week or so, sir."

"That's fine. Today is Wednesday. Let's say the next Wednesday at ten o'clock in the morning."

"That's perfect time, sir. Thank you."

"See you next Wednesday, Jacob." Rabbi Korinetz hung up.

Jacob sighed. It would be a difficult conversation, he thought. Before I'll ask the rabbi for his blessing to marry his daughter, I must tell him the truth about me; the whole truth.

Then Jacob called to book an airline ticket. This time he took an economy class; a business class was too expensive to be paid from his own pocket. The betraying thought that O'Burke was right and that he wouldn't be able to allow himself to resign had come to his mind. How could he start a new life without having a permanent income? Literary royalties? Jacob grinned. Dream and you'll be happy.

For almost an entire week Jacob couldn't pull himself together. Every morning he went to his office, but could not concentrate on the folders needed to be complete that lay before him, closed. Without evidence, there was no cause to investigate, he thought; no investigation, no evidence. It was a vicious circle. Jacob felt as if someone had shut off his ability to analyze a situation.

Only by talking to his devoted friend, his dog Charley, could Jacob regain himself. Sensing his mood, the dog did what he could to cheer his master; he didn't bark. The dog looked at Jacob with his clever, everything-understanding eyes and kept silent as if he wanted to say that in friendship, silence was the highest level of understanding.

Several times Jacob tried to concentrate on the papers that his father had given him to read, but he couldn't; Moses' thoughts seemed too complicated. Only one of the papers seemed him interesting. It was a draft copy of one of the chapters of Moses' memoirs. Jacob read:

After graduating from medical school, being a young, ideal- istic doctor, I joined the Peace Corpus and was sent to a remote village in India. It was the first time that I met a man with an illuminated mind.

The man was very old, so ancient that none of the village inhabitants could say how old he was. Not to mention that he was uneducated. I was called to treat him. But the man was not sick; he was simply too old to live any more. I intended to give him an injection, some vitamins to help him to regain his strength, but the man smiled weakly and said he needed noth- ing as tomorrow he would depart. But as his gratitude for my attempt at taking care of him, he told me a story that I always recall when I hear something about an illuminated mind.

It seems that during the early days in India, a very wise old man always sat by the roadside where pilgrims constantly passed on their way to the tomb of a great saint.

One day a disciple argued that perhaps he could become illu- minated much more quickly if rather than sitting in silence, he join the parade of pilgrims, and he did so.

Within a few months, the disciple returned, very humbled. He seated himself beside the old sage and announced loudly that he was wrong in his belief that only the ground on which his wise, old teacher sat was sacred and holy. But the old teacher said, "God is omnipresent, therefore all ground is holy and sacred, but it depends upon your realization of His presence, and that is in you, my son."

It took me a long time before the real meaning of this story took hold, but when it did, I saw the difference of things in this world. And what was amazing for me was that this old Hindu tale was in a strict accordance with the Kabbalah that I just began to study at that time, still not having the right to do it as I was young, unmarried and without children. All those criteria I satisfied later. I understood later that every Jew studying Kabbalah had an illuminated mind; a mind illuminated by God.

Jacob put Moses' manuscript down and thought that he hadn't known about this fact of his father's biography; the events had place before he was born. He thought that his father's life was not as direct as the lives of most Orthodox Jews. Obviously in my stupid search for self-confirmation, I took after my dad, Jacob thought. He smiled as a wave of warm feelings toward his father seized him.

That evening he went to the synagogue and joined the people reading a weekly chapter of the Torah. It turned out a *geftorah* from the book Bereishit/ Genesis:

God looked over all that He had made, and indeed it was very good.

The rabbi explained that the words **'it was good'** were not said on the second day of creation because that is when death was created. "But the words **'it was very good'** were also appropriate for the second day. Why so?" the rabbi asked. "Because everyone knows that they eventually will die and return to dust. Many repent and return to their Master and are afraid to sin before Him, due to their fear of death. Many fear the King because the sin strips their hands before them and it makes them into good and upright people, and they mend their ways properly. Therefore death is called "**very good**."

Jacob heard the rabbi's explanations with increased interest.

If death is good, he thought, it totally changes the picture of Rabbi Lieberman's death.

"'**And indeed it was good**' is the angel of life; '**very good**' is the angel of death who is even more important than the angel of life," the rabbi said. "Why so? The angel of death's work is to strip the body from its flesh and blood; from the garment of its sins. As soon as the physical body is stripped away, it will be clothed in a spiritual garment in order to reach Gan Eden. And who caused the soul to become clothed in that spiritual garment? The angel of death. Accordingly, the angel of death is very good!" the rabbi finished his explanations.

Jacob felt himself cozy among all the people around him. When he left the synagogue, his feelings of disharmony with the world had vanished. He knew that what he was about to learn would at once surprise him far more than anything he had already discovered.

37.

Jacob's seat in the plane was in the middle of the row. On his left hand there was a young lady with a newborn on her hands. The baby had cried nonstop since the plane took off. On his right hand there was a very stout man, who could hardly squeeze his body in the too narrow for him airline seat. Obviously the man had problems with his bladder as every half an hour he politely said, 'I beg your pardon for disturbing you." After an almost twenty-four hour flight, Jacob was so exhausted that he felt more dead than alive.

His suffering finished only when the plane landed. Jacob whispered a short prayer, unbuckled his seat belt, and wished his fellow travelers a safe way home.

He stayed at the same hotel as before. When he checked in, the clerk recognized him.

"Welcome to Australia again, sir. I remembered you when you've stayed at our hotel the last time. As you're back, it means you liked our country."

"I like your country." Jacob smiled him. "I like the people who live here." He picked up the key from his room and went to the elevator.

*

At ten o'clock in the morning, Jacob rang the bell on the Korinetz house door. To his surprise, the rabbi opened it himself. At seeing Jacob in a formal black suit, the rabbi grinned.

"Hello, detective. I've waited for you. Let's go to my office, please. I am here alone. I've sent all my women to my wife's sister house for six days."

Jacob wanted to say 'good morning, rabbi,' but felt a lump in his throat. He swallowed and followed the rabbi silently. His mood plummeted without reason.

Rabbi Korinetz sat at his desk and showed Jacob to a chair in front of him. Jacob sat and again wanted to say 'thank you, sir,' but again could not. He already hated himself for his silence.

"Don't be surprised, detective. I have known who you were from the beginning, although it was amazing to talk to you about Orthodox Judaism." The rabbi paused. Then he added, "Your father, a pure soul, has told me everything about you. I have to say that your intention to bring me to justice was understandable as living in the material world, people must submit to its laws."

"We all learn by our mistakes in order not to repeat them," Jacob said at last as he regained his ability to talk. "For the last few months, with my father's help, I have understood more than for the last few decades."

"Dr. Reterseil is a great teacher," Rabbi Korinetz agreed. Then he changed the topic. "Anyway, Jacob, you've seen the letter *alef* on Rabbi Lieberman's chest, yes?"

"Yes, sir. I couldn't understand why it was the letter *alef*. Several days ago my father explained that it was the last letter of the Hebrew word 'sin.'"

"The sin," Rabbi Korinetz whispered. "Yes, it was my sin."

"Why it was yours, sir?"

The rabbi glanced at Jacob as if he had only noticed him at that moment.

"It was my sin," he repeated. For an instant he looked through Jacob, not seeing him. Then he was back to the reality. "The mysteries of the Torah are bottomless," he said. "Rabbi Lieberman and I had found the way to repeat Moshe de Leon's discovery of how to join a *tzaddik's* soul. But we were not a 100% sure if it worked. So we had decided to check it out with our own souls before we tried to fulfill Rabbi Lieberman's wish to join Mimonidis' soul. Dr. Reterseil was wrong when he called it a "transfusion of souls." Transfusion means exchanging. We didn't intend to exchange our souls. Only God can do that. If a man tried to do it, it would be a crime as someone could intentionally take a pure soul instead of a soiled one." Rabbi Korinetz made a pause. As Jacob didn't interrupt it, he continued, "In our experiment, I intended to join Rabbi Lieberman's soul, but he insisted on joining mine. Alas, my soul was rejected as it wasn't as pure as Rabbi Lieberman's. That was my sin, and that's my guilt." Rabbi Korinetz paused again and looked at Jacob sadly. "All of us carry our own guilt, detective. We all consider our souls pure, but they are not. Even at the moment of our happiness, we make other people unhappy. That's our guilt," the rabbi repeated.

"Rabbi, nobody can judge you; and I can less than others." Jacob sighed.

"Nobody but God," Rabbi Korinetz said thoughtfully. He again looked at Jacob, but Jacob felt the rabbi did not see him.

"Today I've not come to judge you, rabbi. I am going

to quit my job as a police detective. Today's visit is totally personal, sir…"

Rabbi Korinetz looked at his watch and interrupted Jacob.

"Would you kindly wait for me in the adjacent room, Jacob? I need some time for a prayer."

"Of course, sir," Jacob said, still feeling himself very uncomfortable.

He headed to the door, but on the threshold he glanced back. The rabbi had already begun putting his *tefillin* on…

Jacob went to the adjacent room and sat in the chair, full of thoughts about the upcoming talk with the rabbi. The rabbi must understand that Jacob loves his daughter. They both have the right to be happy, and they need only the rabbi's blessing to achieve that happiness…

Submerged in his thoughts, Jacob didn't know how much time had passed until he heard the wall clock chime the hour. He shuddered and looked at the clock. Obviously half an hour had passed. That was quite enough for a morning prayer, Jacob thought, but he heard no noise from behind the door. Jacob sighed and read a short prayer also.

After the clock chimed a second time, Jacob decided to knock at the rabbi's office door. Nobody answered. He knocked again. The response was the same, silence.

Jacob opened the door quietly, but he didn't see Rabbi Korinetz at his desk. His chair was empty. Jacob did not immediately realize that something had happened. Rabbi Korinetz was not in his study. He couldn't leave the room as the office had the only door, and Jacob had been outside it. *The rabbi had disappeared.*

Jacob went closer to the desk. The Torah lay open on the

desk, the rabbi's *tefillin* lay on the chair; the rabbi's suit lay nearby as if someone had carefully removed the rabbi from it. Jacob shuddered when he saw a small pile of ash on the chair. Only then did Jacob realize that this ash was everything that remained of the rabbi's body. He had burnt his flesh, sending his soul to God for His judgment. He did it without the help of the Angel of Death. How did he do it? Jacob wondered sadly. Obviously nobody would ever know this mystery. Maybe the rabbi was the only one who had ever penetrated this mystery.

Full of sad thoughts, Jacob took the open book in his hand. It was not the Torah, but rather the *Kabbalah*. He whispered the words on the last page that Rabbi Korintz had read.

"The most limiting feature of all is the limitation of time. The limitation of time means that one object cannot be here and somewhere else simultaneously. Moreover, the concept of time is bound up with change. This means that when one thing ceased to be and another thing begins to be, a change has occurred. Change can only take place where the unity and infinity of God are hidden, where the continuity of being is not evident..."

How could Rabbi Korinetz use these words for the act he had just performed? Mysteries, mysteries, mysteries...all our life is a mystery, Jacob thought sadly and sighed deeply. Why had Rabbi Korinetz waited until I arrived to his office to perform this act? Why did he make me a witness? If he carried his guilt after Rabbi Lieberman's death, why didn't he release his soul before?

Jacob turned the page.

"The kelipah (evil) conceals within it a spark of holiness,

which is the vital force of virtue by which the kelipah exists, analogous to a fruit surrounded by a shell. In order to release the holy spark, the encumbering shell must be removed."

What Rabbi Korinetz had done was that he had released the holy spark of his soul and sent it to God, Jacob thought. Suddenly he realized why Rabbi Korinetz had performed it in his presence. He wanted to place his guilt on Jacob's shoulders. Maybe it was Jacob who had pushed him to do it.

Jacob went to the phone to call the police. But at the last moment he changed his mind. What could he tell them? That the rabbi stripped his soul from his body and sent it to God?

Suddenly Jacob remembered the rabbi's words that he had sent his wife and daughter to a relative's house to stay for six days. Why had he said exactly, *for six days*? Not for one; not for two; for six. It meant that he knew that if God forgave him, He would again blow life into the rabbi's dust within six days. The six days of creation!

Jacob sat for a long moment with the receiver in his hand. Then he lowered it. Maybe in six days, when the rabbi's wife and daughter returned home, they would see Rabbi Korinetz sitting at the same place, at his desk, reading the Torah. Maybe in six days God would blow life into the ashes. Everything may be in the mystery of human life, Jacob thought quietly as he closed the door behind him.

The End

ABOUT THE AUTHOR

EDWARD SCHWARTZ is the author of fifteen books written in a wide literary diapason. He graduated from the College of Naval Architecture of St. Petersburg University (Russia) where he earned his M.S. in Engineering and Ph.D. in Physics.

Edward Schwartz currently resides in New York with his family. You can meet him by visiting his Web site at edward-schwartz.com